ZIGZAG THROUGH THE BITTER-ORANGE TREES

ZIGZAG THROUGH THE BITTER-ORANGE TREES

BY ERSI SOTIROPOULOS
Translated from the Greek by Peter Green

Interlink Books

An imprint of Interlink Publishing Group, Inc.
Northampton, Massachusetts

First published in 2007 by

INTERLINK BOOKS
An imprint of Interlink Publishing Group, Inc.
46 Crosby Street, Northampton, Massachusetts 01060
www.interlinkbooks.com

Library of Congress Cataloging-in-Publication Data
Soteropoulou, Erse, 1953–
[Zig-zag stis nerantzies. English]
Zigzag through the bitter orange trees / by Ersi Sotiropoulos ;
translated from the Greek by Peter Green.
p. cm.
ISBN-13: 978-1-56656-661-2 (hardcover)
ISBN-10: 1-56656-661-4 (hardcover)
I. Green, Peter, 1924– II. Title.
PA5630.O825Z5413 2006
889'.334—dc22
2006014161

Printed and bound in the United States of America

To request our complete 40-page full-color catalog,
please call us toll free at **1-800-238-LINK,** visit our
website at **www.interlinkbooks.com,** or write to
Interlink Publishing
46 Crosby Street, Northampton, MA 01060
e-mail: info@interlinkbooks.com

For P.I.I.

still your slave

*T*he phone never stopped ringing: the one thing he remembered about that afternoon. Sleep had overtaken him on the sofa, and he'd slept heavily—no dreams. The phone rang again and again, an insistent hammering note that opened holes in the warm, muggy air. The noise had filled the room, drilled through his skull; he felt the pressure on his temples, and afterward a release, as the ringing faded, like the unwinding of a spring. Then, suddenly, it stopped. Dead silence. And started up again. When he felt the hammering getting near once more, he got up and tried to figure out where the noise was coming from.

He picked up the receiver and answered mechanically. Someone with a nasal voice was trying to get the office of Horizon Movers. He was in no mood for being pushed into a fight, but the guy persisted. Sounding like a pissed-off rooster. What phone number was this, was he quite sure the last figure wasn't zero, oh the hell with it, the moving company must have changed location, couldn't he just take a look in the phone book and come up with the right number? Finally Sid told him to get lost, went back to the sofa, curled up, and that was that.

It was a sultry day, and he was finding it an effort to breathe. His arms hung from his shoulders like foreign bodies. What, he asked himself, was that? Standing there in front of the bathroom mirror. The naked bulb gave off a harsh light with iridescent reflections that seemed to stick in the tiny wrinkles around his mouth. Swollen eyelids, unshaven cheeks, a still-youthful face. No, not youthful: childish. The lower lip making a U. I'm going straight from childhood to middle age, he reflected. And then? Then what? There was no then. Only a need to burp. He hadn't eaten since the evening before, and yet he felt this enormous burp coming up from his stomach into his gullet. A noisy, stinking burp that had been working its way around his innards for hours, and was ready to erupt. That was what. Something stirred behind his back, with a musty flutter of wings.

"Hi there, Maria," said the mynah bird.

It was hanging from the bar in the doorway, and stared at him pop-eyed, as if it had never seen him before.

He got a beer out of the refrigerator and sat down in front of the television. The weekend's score stood at forty-five dead. Corpses one-hundred percent dead, with fine gold chains at their throats and bloodstained scarves, ambulances, sirens screaming, smashed-up cars and a baby-seat tossed out to pasture in the middle of the asphalt. The same images being paraded on every channel. Again and again. Two youths crossed the screen seven times, very carefully carrying a hairy male hand in a nylon bag, and every time they reached the edge of the road they stopped and began chatting with the reporters, making a great thing of their trophy. Sid couldn't have cared less. If he'd been watching the news with some chick, he'd have said, trying to shock her, "They should have stayed home." She'd turn and give him that special look, narrowing her eyes and squinting a little, as if she were trying to thread a needle. He'd keep up his commentary—"Why do they bother with holidays?"— sensing that he was getting near his goal. Afterward he would go out into the hall and order a pizza, and when he got back to his room, the girl would have kicked off her shoes and be humming a tune as she watched MTV.

With the third beer he felt better. His stomach settled back into place, the burp had begun to dissolve, to be absorbed by his deep inner cells. On the TV screen a suntanned fifty-year-old in a yellow blazer was showing a number of guests around a fountain with plastic lilies, and before letting them sit down introduced each of them, with extravagant and ridiculous gesticulation. If I can hit the yellow blazer, Sid said, I'll get up for a beer. He spat.

The gob flew screenward and stuck there, an inch or two under its target, like a squashed maggot. Are you ever off form, he told himself. If I hit the fountain I won't have another drink, he said, and spat again. Bingo!

"Hi there, Maria," said the mynah.
"Hi there, Maria," he told it.

In the evening the phone calls began again. It wasn't the same voice as in the afternoon, of that he was sure. The caller knew his name, or, more likely, had picked it at random from the phone book. He spoke politely, in a flat sing-song tone, and kept on about something persistently. But his diction was incomprehensible, and Sid hung up. The phone rang again. "Can we intelest you in subscliling to..."

Finally he got it. A Chinaman was trying to sign him up for the local newspaper. Could you believe it?

Intelest.
Subsclibing...
Tomorrow.

Late that night it began to rain: a cleansing downpour that fell with a steady roar from the burst clouds. Sid didn't hear the rain. In his sleep he sensed the unexpected coolness stealing into the room and spreading out like a cold compress over the baking walls. He felt an airy sprite approach and stroke his forehead. He didn't hear the mynah bird frantically beating its wings inside its cage. He didn't hear the shutters banging, or the rush of water in the storm drains. It rained and rained. The city flushed itself out.

Lia was woken by the rain, and propped herself up on her elbows. The windows were curtainless, and the spectacle of water beating fiercely against the panes suddenly brought back the flavor of a long-lost morning. *Love me, love me tender...* Who'd said that? It was a song. One morning when she and some other girls had played hooky and gone to the seaside. June—no, May, because it was still chilly. Walking under a cloudy sky they'd met three fishermen and pretended they were American kids. "Fishes, fishes, we want fishes," Fifi had shouted, scampering barefoot along the beach. She'd taken off her school pinafore and hitched up her skirt around her waist, showing off her famous legs. Her nickname was the Octopus Diva. The fishermen were entranced, and gave her a basketful of red mullet. And after that? After that it started raining and they all got soaked. *Love me tender,* went the transistor, with a wailing note from a saxophone at the end of the refrain.

There were six beds in the ward, but hers was the only occupied one. The last patient had been discharged the previous afternoon. It was so marvelous being left on her own, listening to the noise the water made as it roared down the gutter. Love me, love me, sucker. But there was something else, too. Water in the fish soup—when was that? She couldn't recall. A child bending his head over his plate as though they'd given him a scolding. Maybe he's crying? Yes, he's crying, tears dropping into the fish soup. But that's not it, or not all of it. There's rainwater in the fish soup, no doubt about it. A veranda with geraniums, and a set table. They're spending the summer in the country, it's late August. Her brother with his clean-shaven scalp. He takes a spoonful of soup and spits it back into the plate. Someone smacks him. And then the rain starts. All the rest pick up their plates and run indoors. Her brother stays there, nailed to his chair, head bent over the fish soup. His narrow shoulders shake with his sobs, while the rain forms a thin trickle running down from hairline to nose, and dripping into the soup bowl.

And what else? What else? Go on, say it. Bodies emerging from a sleepless night and walking for a while side by side without a word spoken. Dawn has broken, and they sway slightly, realizing, in this first light, that the other body is not their own. Leaving a night's lovemaking behind, both taking away their own share of skin. Bodies that advance without moving as it begins to rain. What's been written into the skin cannot be erased, they're thinking. The mornings pile up. How many such mornings exist in the course of a life? Three, four, maybe ten at most. Always the same. Trying to keep your skin in place. Walking in the rain out of sheer inertia.

The rain had eased up. Very soon the nurses would be doing their rounds. Today the Prize Student was on duty—a coarse-featured youth with a stupid short-sighted stare. And white clogs that echoed all the way down the corridor. But how can I know? How is it that I remember that scene, and no other: my brother hunched over his bowl and crying in the rain? I was inside. I was eating. I detested fish soup, but after what had happened I dared not protest. I could see his back, his heaving shoulders, and I could imagine, only too well, the fury and despair caged in that small body. Imagine it, not see it. I was sitting near the window. I could see the rain lashing the geraniums, the earth swelling, turning into mud. I could imagine that he was unhappy. I was capable of knowing this, not imagining it. I could have known. I didn't want to know. Why not? I was a little kid, and scared. A lie. I was capable of knowing, but I didn't want to.

"What a terrible storm, good morning," said the cleaning woman as she came in. She picked up the wastebasket to empty it, and looked around in a preoccupied way. The angry stomp of clogs could be heard approaching from the next ward.

"*Idiota Furioso.*"

"What?" asked the cleaning woman.

Nothing, nothing. She shook her head.

"Good morning, good morning, just as well it's cooled off, right?"

Right, dummy. He was pushing the trolley in front of him; he left it beside the bed and, without looking at her, began to prepare the syringe, the butterfly needle, and the rubber tourniquet for taking a blood sample from her.

"Could you please ask someone else to do this?"

He stared at her from behind his thick glasses as though seeing an extraterrestrial.

"I can do anything anyone else can," he snarled impatiently.

"My arm bruised black and blue last time."

"Let me do my job." He bent over her, holding the rubber tourniquet, ready to tie it around her arm. "I know exactly where the vein is—"

"No!" She jumped out of bed and ran barefoot to the bathroom, dragging the I.V. drip with its stand behind her.

It was a small room, warm and damp, that smelled of something indefinable, not chlorine, not alcohol, but some out-of-date and forgotten odor, which had permeated the walls and was now evaporating, leaving its imprint behind. The steamy atmosphere of a Turkish bath. It was always nice to come in here and be on her own for a bit. Outside she heard the loud tones of the nurse, who'd made for the physicians' office and was lodging a complaint. Yap yap yap. Usually there were three bedpans on the tiled floor of the shower. Today one was missing. Must be some new bedridden patient. There was no soap or toilet paper, each patient supplied her own. "Nobody loves us, so hospitals are just the place for us," she'd sometimes say when she had friends visit and wanted to amuse them. At first the laughs would be a little forced: some found her eccentric, while others suspected a serious problem with her health. Then she'd raise the stakes, bluff. She'd say how great it is when you're ill, that a fever gives you the best high of all, and that the wildest sex happens right after surgery when you're still dopey from the anaesthetic. And that once, in the intensive-care unit, she'd seen a two-headed penis—"A two-headed penis! At last!" a woman gallery owner exclaimed at this, after which she abruptly lapsed into a catatonic silence.

Hmm. Her friends were beginning to get bored. Hmm. Hmm. Some hangers-on tagged along to begin with because they didn't have anything better to do, and kept on because it was all free entertainment. But she didn't really know how to bluff. She wasn't a good poker player, that she did know. And her friends, one after the other, were beginning to slip away.

In the meantime—

Someone was knocking at the bathroom door.

Professor Kalotychos, very stiff and exasperated.

Come out of there.

You're not a child.

All this is nonsense.

And how are you going to see the new millennium in, Sid?

With a beer in one hand and my prick in the other.

Hee-hee.

Say that again?

Screw you.

But what they enjoyed most were the anecdotes about her little brother. Three years younger than her, real sharp, with a rib-cracking sense of humor. Black, *très noir*. Never went out before dark. Lived by himself with a mynah bird. Was unpredictable. Red, yellow, blue, the whole spectrum. And once, during a religious procession, when some black-suited prime minister or other was marching along arm in arm with a bunch of bishops, her brother, five years old at the time, had gone up to the top floor of the house and peed on the parade.

Say that again?

· 2 ·

*I*f I was an American hero," Sid said, "I'd know what to do." He eyed the crowd, searching for his next words. People had begun to arrive in droves. They went into the bar, got a drink, and then came back to the sidewalk and stood there, jammed close together, conversing in loud voices, with gestures.

"See that chick?" P. said. "I'm imagining her on the phone, in the dark, naked."

Sid turned around. The girl was dancing by herself. She was thin and narrow-faced. There were colored spotlights hidden in the trees, their beams crossing diagonally at the side of the street. Sid saw her face flinch as it passed through the cone of lights, and then watched some tall oaf in a white shirt go up to her, catch her by the waist, and swing her off her feet.

"All right," P. said, "what would you do?" Yeah, what? The girl's face turned mauve and then, abruptly, red, the face of a pantomime demon. "If you were an American hero?" Oh. I'd know what to do. I'd say I had to turn my life around, that it was high time for me to take to the streets, or the hills—Crap. Bullshit. "Well?" P. insisted.

"Watch this," Sid said, and took off. The idea he had was to go and get into conversation with the girl and bring her over to P., but as he struggled to make his way through the crowd he began to have doubts. Someone pushed him, and half his beer slopped over his sleeve. "Watch out, jerk," said the guy. "You talking to me?" Sid asked him. He was a skinny thin-lipped guy, with big teeth. "You talking to me?" Sid repeated. He felt his collar sticking to his skin. But the moving crush of people had carried him on, and the skinny guy had vanished. He looked back and saw P. standing with his back against the tree trunk, watching him with an enigmatic smile.

Sid stepped off the sidewalk and moved toward the spotlights. He couldn't see the girl anywhere. The tall oaf with the white shirt was smoking, one foot resting nonchalantly on the foot pedal of an Africa Twin. There was a baldy standing beside him, a baldy with glazed eyes and a fishface like a bream's. Sid followed his gaze and saw her. She was standing between two parked cars, swaying to and fro, chin sunk on her chest, shoulders raised like wings. Sid stopped a step or two away from her, and tried to command his body to relax. *"Black magic woman—"* Where had they dug that one up? *"Like a black magic woman—"* Again he tried to issue a command to his body: to dance. He took a step toward the girl, snapping his hands rhythmically. She didn't seem to have noticed him. "Daba dooba daba," he went, in the rhythm of the song. He came closer to her. The space between the cars was very narrow. He leaned on the hood and put his mouth to her ear. "Daba dooba," he intoned. The girl raised her head and stared at him like a deaf-mute. Her scent, of decaying jasmine, was very pungent, and he drew back a little, letting the air circulate between them.

"You don't speak African?" he asked pompously.

"Sorry?" Her gaze widened, as if it were part of her effort to hear better.

"Daba dooba!" Sid yelled.

"What's that jerk after?" the tall oaf asked, pushing up onto both feet.

"Daba dooba," Sid repeated.

"A finger up his ass, that's what," sniggered the fishface with the glazed eyes.

The girl made a gesture indicating "Oh, he's crazy," and started dancing again.

Ten yards separated him from the Africa Twin. Ten yards means half a minute. Three minutes, if you're going to a funeral. Sid glanced back to see what P. was doing, but a whole new group of people had taken up position in front of the tree, their faces flickering among the leaves, as the red beam caught them, like some strange fruit. Two minutes, he figured, and set off. The tall oaf glanced at fishface, and fishface shook his head. In every movie there's a scene where you see the hero walking purposefully. He has an objective, and nothing can stop him. He strides on, looking straight ahead. Does he feel ridiculous? I don't think so. If he felt ridiculous he'd turn back. Sid became aware that he'd started to slacken his pace. Where are you, P.? he wondered, and felt the sweat sticky on his neck. Tall oaf and fishface were watching his progress in silence. "Daba dooba," whispered Sid. He saw two more guys sidling over to the Africa Twin, as though someone had signaled them that something was up.

But he still had some ground to cover. Slow motion, that was the gimmick. The hero has time to consider. He's moving forward, but his feet are taking him back. Back where? To various happenings. Sid saw that the girl had gone up to the tall oaf and was telling him something, with an uneasy air. Daba dooba. The hero has time to consider small incidents. Half-finished or self-contained episodes. Those that determined today's outcome. That led him into this mess. Daba dooba. The hero goes back. And gets there.

"Look at that jerk, how he's shaking," said the tall oaf.

Fishface shrugged. "So?"

There were now five of them, including the girl. They watched him with curiosity, as though observing the struggles of a larva in its cocoon.

"Cuckoo," said Sid.

"Cuckoo..." the tall oaf mimicked him, in a flat voice, and then burst out laughing.

Sid tried to hold his body erect, but this was

becoming steadily harder. Now he had got this far he wanted to say something more. Something to make them remember him. But his mind was vacant. "Bye, now," he mumbled. Then he turned and fled.

Sid.
Isidore Vicious.
Here.

"So what's up, bro?"
"Everything's OK, bro."

The moment he put down the receiver he felt uneasy. He opened the refrigerator and stood staring into its lighted interior. They'd talked about the rain: she'd done the talking. She'd said it was fantastic, that she'd enjoyed it as much as reading an Agatha Christie whodunit. The rain like an Agatha Christie whodunit? His sister was always coming out with remarks like that. They hadn't said anything else. But she'd seemed somehow—somehow artificially cheerful. Bright and perky, but hitting the wrong note. He shut the refrigerator and decided to go to the hospital.

He got there a quarter of an hour before visiting hours began. In the hospital courtyard there was a canteen, and one or two benches set here and there among the bitter-orange trees. He ordered a toasted sandwich and sat down to wait. Two old men in pajamas were sitting on the bench across from him, chatting.

"Money for old rope, I'm telling you," one of them was saying. He'd forgotten to put in his dentures, and was spraying saliva as he spoke. "My brother-in-law made twenty thousand off his shares in Delos Insurance."

The other man shook his head incredulously.

"What's the matter, you don't believe me?" the toothless guy snapped.

"I've heard that Titan Cement stocks are doing very nicely," his companion ventured. He had a catheter, and was holding the bag tight in one hand.

"Titan Cement? I haven't got time for such crap," said the first man, and flourished one arm in the air as though chasing off a fly. He gazed out despondently in front of him, and began chewing at his gums.

Two nurses strolled by, one of them pushing an empty wheelchair.

After a moment one of the men said, with a sigh, glancing indifferently at Sid as he spoke, "God, it's hot."

"Let me tell you," the other replied, "it's not just hot, it's a real scorcher."

And both of them relapsed into silence.

Lia was sitting in a chair beside her bed with the I.V. drip stand next to her. She didn't hear him come in: she was absorbed by something, very likely the pattern on her nightgown. She looked smaller to him, as though she'd shrunk since last time. "Hi, bro," he said, and kissed her.

So?

Everything under control.

A nurse came in with her tray. He'd forgotten that they ate so early in hospitals.

"Remember when Sissy was born, and we went to the clinic to see her, and they gave us a present, a box of paper cut-outs that Sissy was supposed to have brought us, and at some point they brought in Mom's meal, baked fish, something we'd never liked, but that day we began a fight over who was going to get to eat it—?"

"No, I don't," Sid said, and meant it. He couldn't figure out what his sister was getting at.

"Don't you remember how while we were fighting Mom had some kind of attack, toxic convulsions I think, and they hurried us out of the room without telling us anything, and doctors kept coming and going all that night, and she almost died?"

"I'd forgotten that," he lied. In fact he couldn't recall any of it, but he looked at her as though he understood, and was curious to know why she was bringing it up now.

"Mom said later that it was the first time the two of us had fought—I mean, after Sissy was born," Lia went on. She was extremely tense.

"What's that got to do with it?" Sid asked. He was beginning to get irritated. This happened every time the conversation went somewhere he wasn't expecting.

Lia eyed him quizzically. "Oh, great, are you that dumb?"

Could she be beginning to lose it? Sid wondered.

"Are you that dumb?" she repeated impatiently.

"The tray, look at it!"

"Baked fish—"

"—that smells like—"

"—shit on your shoes!"

"Bravo!" said Lia, bouncing up and down. "Now take that tray and get it out of here this instant."

OK. That makes sense. Sid found a nurse in the corridor and gave her the tray. From her expression he realized that his sister often made a fuss about the food. "She's very sick," he said, trying to make excuses for her. The woman said nothing, just marched off with the tray.

Left alone in the room, Lia reflected that it would have been better if Sid hadn't come. She was the one who had to make all the effort, keep inventing. Topics of conversation run out. Sissy's birth, baked fish, shit on your shoes. And what else after that? Inevitably they'd get on to Dr. Kalotychos. She felt a kind of nervous exhaustion at the prospect. Sid was going to be forced to play a role he didn't know, a role he detested. The brother, the guardian angel.

"Want to go for a walk?" he asked as he came back into the room.

She shook her head.

I'll tell him about the Prize Student, she thought. The moment this idea struck her she felt relieved. "I need your help—" she began. Sid stared at her questioningly. What was coming now? "There's this new nurse—" she went on in a rush, and plunged into the story, highlighting all the details: syringes, ruptured veins, his banging his fist on the medical trolley, and the rest of it. "You know what he did to me last Saturday?"

"No," Sid muttered. He was feeling a kind of limp apprehension.

"Well, listen to this. They turn the lights out at nine. All that's left on is a single, low-power, green nightlight in each ward. Well, he fixed the system. Saturday evening was his shift. The moment they threw the main switch, this ward lit up like, like Easter, like a firework display, do you understand?"

"No."

"I spent the whole night under operating theater lights. There was no way they could turn them off."

"OK, what did you do?"

"I knew you'd ask that. I kept ringing the nurses' bell. He played dumb. Finally the head nurse showed up. She said there was a fault in the electrical circuit, there was nothing she could do about it. We just had to wait till morning. I spent that whole night like some worm, eyes wide open under an interrogator's searchlight. It was him, I know it was." She paused a moment, then said: "I want you to pay him back." Her eyes glinted. She made them glint.

"Are you in love, maybe?"

"You don't understand anything."

Sid glanced at the wall to see if there was a clock there.

"What about the mynah bird?" she asked.

"I've got to get rid of it."

He looked around again for a clock. How long were visiting hours here? A black bird went by outside the window, made a complete circle, and vanished. From the corridor came a clatter of plates.

Dirty cutlery dropping with a metallic jingle into a tin bowl. A trolley was wheeled past, squeaking, and stopped at the next ward. They were collecting the trays. "I saw Kalotychos," he said, softly, as though afraid someone might hear him. "I didn't speak to him—he was just going into his office," he added, anticipating her question. Instantly he felt uncomfortable.

Lia appeared calm, almost indifferent. She was looking down with great concentration at the patterns on her nightgown. So little, a bundle of bones. He went across and hugged her. "If you need anything, just let me know, OK?"

So?
Everything under control.

In the courtyard the old men had spread a pack of cards over a cardboard boxtop and were playing solitaire. A nurse was standing smoking by one of the bitter-orange trees, with a full plastic cup of Nescafé in her free hand. "You got the time?" she asked him as he went by her.

Sid shook his head, smiling.

Nurses and maids: another chapter in the Lia story. As he moved forward, he tripped. There was a crossing for the disabled, where the concrete dipped in a curve to let the wheelchairs go up. He lost his balance. The hero marches straight forward and stumbles. He falls and gets up again. And suddenly he remembered everything. What a miserable, wretched creature. Their mother was very young then, younger than he was now. A childlike face, a U-shaped chin, petite. Big tits. Ssshh!

Big tits. Oh hush. She was nursing Sissy, trying to breast-feed the little monster. Their father was pacing round her room in the clinic, a bunch of nerves ready to explode. Lia and he were at the end of the bed. That was when the tray came in. Baked fish, yes. Up to that point she'd told it straight. And they certainly hadn't noticed the fish. They were making cardboard cut-outs with the present Sissy was supposed to have brought them from the other world. They were a bit bored. Very bored. "Want me to make you look beautiful?" Lia suddenly asked him. "Sure." They went into the bathroom. No one paid any attention to them. Lia started cutting his hair. The sink filled up with tufts. "Now you look beautiful," she told him. Then they came back into the bedroom.

God all fucking mighty! Their father exploded straight into the heavens that had sent Sissy.

For fuck's sake—

I ask you, are these creatures children?

Calm down, please. The baby—

What were you up to in there? How could you let her do that to you, huh? You moron, you dummy—

Please calm down—

Fuck it all to hell.

"You jerk, where were you?" P. asked.

"My sister, jerk. I've got to get her out of that place."

· 21 ·

"I saw the chick."

"Black Magic?"

"Yep."

"Tell me."

"You've got it made, big boy. Did you say cuckoo or something like that to her?

"Daba dooba."

"She wants to meet you."

· 3 ·

*Y*ou didn't come home for your name day, Sotiris," said Mama Koula. "We were expecting you, I'd even made your favorite garlic sauce—" She eyed her son with pride. He'd grown even taller: a bit gawky, she had to admit, but still a fine, upstanding young man. How could she forget that proud moment on Clean Monday,* the last time he'd visited the village, when he'd let out the string of his kite and it had begun to climb, soaring right over Tamvakoulas's three-story house and into the clouds like a shot from a gun, leaving everyone else's far behind? She'd been very close to tears. Holy Virgin ever vigilant—

"I brought you some sweets," Sotiris said.

"Chocolate mice?" trilled Mama Koula.

Sotiris unwrapped the box. Chocolate mice.

* The first day of Lent in Greece, celebrated with country picnics and kite-flying. *Trans.*

The afternoon light was fading. Across the water the lumpish mass of Mt. Paliovouna turned orange, then gradually pink. "Tomorrow we'll have the Mesolonghi crowd here," Mama Koula said.

Sotiris felt a stab of irritation. He wanted to tell her that she shouldn't have invited them now, while he was here, but he couldn't summon the courage. And it was for his benefit that she'd asked them, he was sure about that.

"Going for a walk, are you?" she asked.

Why did she always have to ask him the same thing? He was going to stay in. He had no friends in the village. He waited till his father came back from the coffeehouse, and then they all settled themselves in front of the television.

"What a shambles," Mama Koula muttered. "Seeing all this now, it might have been better if you hadn't come—"

"Thirty-three people killed." his father announced, as though he'd counted them personally, "not to mention serious injuries—"

"You be careful now," Mama Koula told Sotiris.

"I come on the bus," Sotiris said.

"I mean when you get a car," she insisted.

"Better if he doesn't get one," his father interjected.

"Look, why do they keep showing us that stretcher?"

Laid out on the stretcher was a badly smashed-up woman.

"Mincemeat," his father said.

"She has to be my age, and look what she's

wearing, Bermuda shorts," said Mama Koula. She shook her head.

The woman was middle-aged and chubby. Sotiris stared at the screen unmoved. The images of the mangled bodies and the chattering of the reporters had a soothing effect on him. In the hospital he saw far worse. And there was that halfwitted girl in Ward 11 who kept making trouble for him.

"You look tired," Mama Koula told him. "You want me to make up your bed?"

"I may go out," he decided.

"Fine, go have some fun," they encouraged him.

He waited till it was quite dark before he left the house. He crossed the yard and shut the fence gate carefully behind him. But he didn't go down to the waterfront. The noise from the main road wafted back to him: screaming children, slow-moving cars with their windows open and music blaring. He strolled aimlessly for a while past the one-story houses with their tiny gardens, kicking pebbles as he went. After going all the way around the block he headed for the bottom of the hill, taking his time, breathing deeply. He tried to distinguish the various smells: grass, earth, goats. In a house a long way off he thought he heard a woman singing. A deep, mournful voice. He turned off into a small overgrown road and found himself walking down the middle of a dried-up watercourse. He caught the woman's voice again, coming from some distant point out beyond the fields. It was very dark. He saw a light in the distance, and at the same moment sensed the presence of animals very close to him. Somewhere nearby they must have dug a manure hole.

"Shush," said a man's voice. Sotiris froze. He couldn't make out anything. He heard twigs crackling, as though someone was moving quickly toward him.

"What's going on?" a woman called out. A dim figure materialized in front of him and he tried to hold his breath. But it came no nearer. The man had decided to ferret around in the other direction, behind the house. "Come back in," he heard the woman say, "it wasn't anything, just dogs." Like a sleepwalker, Sotiris turned around and followed the path back. He felt as though he'd stopped breathing. "Who's there?" the man suddenly shouted, within a hair's breadth of colliding with him. He must have circled all the way around the field till they ended up face to face.

Sotiris took to his heels. He got the impression that the man was running after him, but after a little he heard nothing. Just the quiet of the fields. Where was he now? He saw the lights of the waterfront twinkling in the distance and began running toward them. As he came into an inhabited area he tripped over a gas can and his glasses fell off. He didn't stop to retrieve them, just kept on running till he reached his house.

The two rooms and the yard were enveloped in darkness. All he could see through the window was the grainy light of the television, playing with the sound off. He walked up the whitewashed front path, between the pots of basil. Their heavy scent, intensified by the night air, nauseated him. He slid back the latch to the henhouse, ducked his head, and went inside. The hens made a nervous flutter and then settled back down on their perches. He sat down in a corner on the straw, head bowed, arms clasped around his knees, doing his best to calm himself, get his breath back. His heart kept pounding irregularly.

"Leave sheep to shepherds." This was the first thing he heard his father say when he woke up next morning. The Mesolonghi crowd had arrived, and were already digging into the appetizers. As usual, they were talking politics. "Hello, Athenian," they said when they saw him, "come and join us." He stood in the doorway trying to sort out all their faces.

"Sit down," said Mama Koula. "What are you trying to do, grow taller or something?" She was in a cheerful mood.

"Leave sheep to shepherds," his father repeated.

"I lost my glasses." Sotiris said. No one paid any attention to him.

"Good health!" said his father, glass raised.

"Cheers!"

There were six of them, they'd come in a pick-up. His father's relatives. Mama Koula hadn't stopped to breathe, whirling around like a top, cutting bread, filling glasses, every so often wiping the sweat from her forehead with one hand. "I heard a rumor about fish pie," his father said, eyeing her

enquiringly. "Patience," she said. "All in good time."
"Service fit for royalty, eh?" said someone
admiringly. "Cheers!"

By the time the fish pie arrived half of them
were drunk. They'd pushed back the table away
from the sun, and ate with their legs stretched out.
Sotiris was hungry, and didn't talk while eating. His
head was spinning, but without making him feel
sick. It was probably the effort he had to make to
see, to pick up the right piece with his fork. "Come
on, Mama Koula, you sit down too," someone said.

"Leave sheep to shepherds," said his father,
without raising his head from his plate. The words
could mean anything: on this particular occasion,
that the men should sit at table while the women
stood and waited on them.

"Anyone for cards?" somebody asked, mouth
still crammed. There was a general enthusiastic
response. Mama Koula began collecting the dirty
plates. Sotiris slipped out without a word. He had to
look for his glasses.

"Look, Mt. Paliovouna's changing color," said the
younger girl, using her hand as a visor. "I know," said
the older one, without looking. They were sitting on
a bench at the wharf in the old harbor. Nobody went
there any more. There were some fishing boats
moored to the pier, and beyond them an old man
mending his nets. The sun was still high, and it was
hot. "It's just turned pink, you've never seen anything
like it," the younger girl exclaimed impatiently.

"Will you please not bother me?" the big one sighed. She took a magazine from the cloth satchel at her feet, and leafed through it, bored.

The younger girl looked at the mountain directly in front of her. It was changing now from pink to blue, its foothills still deep in shadow. She felt as though a powerful shot of light were streaking from the bare peak straight across the sea, aimed directly at her chest. She closed her eyes and pressed her fingers against her eyelids. Thousands of tiny fireflies flickered under the velvety skin, and her mind became a bright dome that darkened with breathtaking speed. When she opened her eyes, the summit and sides of the mountain had vanished. The light was now a halo around the more distant range and the smaller hills, all dancing in a haze of dust. The shore opposite seemed to be sinking into the water, and suddenly the distance separating the two coastlines shrank by half. The girl picked up a stone and clutched it in her hand. There was a stillness all around: the mixed scent of brine and grilling food hung in the air. She turned her gaze toward the pier, saw a thin column of smoke rising from the old fisherman's skiff, and stood up to get a better view. He'd set up a little gas stove on the prow, and was now keeping an eye on it, hunched over the small flame. She sat down on the bench again, the stone still clenched in her fist, shut her left eye, and started to take aim. The water in front of her was filthy. Big oil stains gleamed on the surface of the sea like discs of light, slowly spreading and changing shape. The girl let the stone drop to the ground and stood up, shaking her legs to get the circulation going.

"What's an Egyptian river with five letters?" the older girl asked after a while.

"The Nile," the younger girl replied, and sat down again beside her, bending across to look at her magazine. She had a thin, nervous face; its intense expression, under her dark tousled hair, gave her a somewhat wild appearance. Despite her tan, her skin seemed pale.

"The Nile has four letters, didn't you even learn how to count?"

"I don't know, leave me alone," the younger girl said. She took another look at Mt. Paliovouna, and after that at the pier in front of her. Two gulls, the only ones left on the landing stage, were advancing side by side along the gangway with little bobbing steps. Every so often, as though by tacit agreement, they would speed up and take off skyward, circle vaguely, and then, both together, dive into the water, surfacing again with nothing except a piece of trash or a melon rind that they'd drop back into the sea. The girl watched them idly for a little. Then she turned away, looked back, and asked: "Got enough money for a shish-kebab?" "No," said her companion, sharply. The younger girl took a Mickey Mouse purse out of her pocket. From it she extracted two worn bills and some change, and began counting the coins. Then she put them back in the purse, zipped it shut, and put it away again.

The aroma of grilling fish had become stronger, as the smoke eddied out from the old man's skiff and slowly reached the waterfront.

"Let's go take a look—maybe it caught fire…"

"What's a three-letter temporal adverb?"

"Now," said the younger girl.

"What a hopeless lump you are," the older girl snapped, and then, almost in the same breath, exclaimed: "Hey, hold on, you're right!" But the younger girl had gotten up and was on her way to the pier.

The old man had a cap on and was bending over, so that his face wasn't visible. He'd lit some newspapers and was grilling a herring. "Hi there, kid," he said when he saw her. She went over to him, curious. "Like to do something really gutsy to help me?" he asked, and at once began explaining what it was she would have to do. He wanted her to help him in setting a trap for the rats that climbed aboard the skiff at night and gnawed through his nets.

"There are rats in the harbor?"

"As big as cats."

He bent down and tried to find the end of a thick coil of rope among the heaps of green nets. The other end of the rope was hitched to some scrap iron, and it took him quite a while to work all the knots loose. "Aah, I'm sick of this," he said when he'd finished, and gave her a sidelong glance from under the peak of his cap.

"What's your name?" he asked.

"Nina."

He threaded one end of the rope through a can with holes in it, and gave it her to hold. "Smart as all get out, those little critters," he grumbled, and for a moment or two he half vanished into the hold of his boat. He dragged out a bit of cardboard, shaped it into a cone, and tried to hold it in place by tying the other end of the rope around it; but the knot slipped and came undone immediately. "Aah, I'm sick of this," he repeated. He tried again, first seeing if he could fix the rope to an old leaky pail, then poking holes with a piece of wire through a plastic bottle, then nailing a bit of lining material onto a rusted frame, until finally he managed it. But he still seemed unsatisfied, and kept on searching under his nets for other accessories to finish off his trap. He was a tiny old man, with crafty slit eyes and a monkey-like face. There was almost no flesh left on him. He showed her how to fix the bait and light the pressure lamp. I'm glad I came and met him, Nina thought.

"And now, if you're a good girl, there's something you'll tell me..."

"All right," she said, and gave him a sideways look.

"Which do you love more, your dad or your mom?"

"I'm an orphan," she said, and stared down at her shoes, feeling the urge to giggle.

"Sorry," he mumbled. "I had no idea."

"Bye, then."

She jumped off the skiff and made her way back, tiptoeing down the walkway on the pier. Now I'm walking along the edge of a terrifying precipice. At every instant I'm in danger of slipping and falling. There are black crows circling threateningly above my head, cawing. Their beaks open and shut in nightmarish shrieks. They're waiting to tear me apart. No one can save me. I'm alone. No one will hear my screams. But I still walk right on the edge. I keep perfect balance and walk on. I go on walking. Perfectly balanced. All the others are idiots and zombies because they can't see this.

When she got back to the wharf the older girl was still doing the crossword. The small one got down on her knees and settled beside her. She stared vaguely at the letters in the little squares, and then turned her head and tried to read the answers on the back page. She switched around and stared behind her. She sensed an inquisitive presence, like a gaze fixed on her back. "Someone's watching us," she said. "Oh, stop your nonsense, we're going home," the bigger girl told her. "Let's stay just a little longer," the younger one pleaded.

She looked carefully around behind her. Except for the old warehouses, there was nothing else in the harbor. The warehouses had been abandoned: only the central building was still standing; the rest were in ruins. Immediately next to the ruins ran a broken fence with wooden posts around which wild oleander grew, and beyond that the reeds began, stretching all the way to the sea. There was nobody there. Yet she had the same feeling again: an observant gaze, scratching at her back. "Someone's watching us," she said again. She turned around and looked again. Something moved in among the oleanders. "Look, there!" she exclaimed, pointing.

"Don't be silly," the big girl said.

"Come with me, let's go look."

The big girl put down her magazine and reluctantly got to her feet. The younger girl raced ahead of her. I was right, she thought when she reached the oleanders. Someone was here a little while ago, but now he's gone. The oleanders had been trampled down, and she saw a still-burning cigarette butt. Someone had been there a long time. Someone who stayed hidden.

When Sotiris got back home, the Mesolonghi crowd were getting ready to leave, and knocking back their last round of ouzo. "Hey, Athenian, what happened, you forget about us?" they all chorused as soon as they saw him come in. There were two small plates of olives and sliced cucumber left on the table. Sotiris fetched a chair from the yard and sat himself down next to them.

"You forgot about us," said Mama Koula, with a deep sigh.

"How d'you suppose you're going to get him married if you never let him loose from your apron strings?" his father said. He seemed pleased with his day. His face was scarlet. His eyes radiated a mellow warmth: he had all of them gathered around him. He looked his son up and down. "What happened to your glasses?"

"I dropped them."

"Did they break?"

"I'll get another pair in Athens."

"That boy has an answer for everything," Mama Koula said.

"That boy's what you made of him. Single-handed."

· 4 ·

Just how P. managed to get a word with Black Magic, Sid had no idea. A mystery. Nor could he figure out any reason why his friend should have interceded on his behalf. He went off to their first meeting in a lighthearted and unquestioning mood. The girl had got to the Banana Moon before him. She was sitting at a small table under a mulberry tree, and hadn't ordered anything. She was smoking a Marlboro.

"Hi there," he said as he reached her, "I'm Sid."

"Hi."

Sid cleared his throat.

"Black Magic, right?"

"Julia."

She had a very narrow, triangular face. A puckish look. She asked for Nescafé with milk and three spoonfuls of sugar: still too early for alcohol, she explained. She had pretty shoulders and small pointed breasts. She wasn't wearing a bra, and if Sid had managed to take a good look, he'd have seen her nipples standing out hard and taut like olive pits.

"I wear contact lenses," she said, as though answering a question.

"Really? I hadn't noticed."

"Everyone says that's the first thing they notice."

They both fell silent. Sid got up to get a second drink. The course he had to follow until enough time had elapsed, after which they'd get up together and he'd suggest their going back to his place, was clearly delineated in his mind's eye. It wouldn't need any great effort, either, of that he was sure. Still, he had to be careful. No more than three drinks. No lunatic theories.

"How are your friends?"

Julia shrugged.

"That tall guy seems really into you."

"He's gay."

"Gay?"

"Yeah, I only hang out with gays," Julia explained. "With gay men, I mean."

The music inside the joint suddenly got louder. Sid, uneasily, sensed a faintly stirring disquiet. The tables around them had already filled up, and new customers were standing waiting beside the bar. The girl was rocking gently to and fro on her chair, vacantly watching the scene. This deal's going wrong, he thought. The prospect of their getting up to dance, or, even worse, of her starting to dance solo, threading her way through the various groups, made him panic.

"You ever seen a mynah bird?" he blurted out suddenly.

"No. A what?" she said, puzzled, and went on moving in time with the music.

"It's something you have absolutely got to see—" he said, caught her by the arm, and, almost violently, pulled her up from her seat. In the taxi they exchanged only a few words. "We live very close to each other," she said when they got there. All the better, he thought. He wouldn't have to see her home afterward. He paid the cabbie and they got out.

The moment he opened the door to his apartment, letting her go in ahead of him, he nearly collapsed. The place was in a complete mess, with all the excitement of his date he'd forgotten to clean it up. And the mynah had got out of its cage and left droppings all over the hall. But Julia didn't seem to notice; she marched straight ahead, calling, "Mynah, mynah, where are you?"

"She'll come out by herself, and she'll decide when," Sid said.

"What's her name?"

Sid hesitated to answer.

"Don't call her," he said, and then: "Her name's Maria."

"Maria, Mareeeah, where are you hiding?" Julia called.

Sid put out two whiskeys and a bowl of potato chips and sat down on the sofa. Julia came over and sat beside him.

"You don't have any rum, do you?" she asked.

"No."

"Just lately I've really had a thing for rum and coke... It doesn't matter," Julia said. She picked up the remote control, and ran through the channels till she found MTV. So far so good, Sid thought. He settled himself back on the couch and put his arm around her shoulders.

"Why were you saying daba dooba to me?" she asked him.

"Because—" Sid strained to make himself absolutely clear—"there's this queen of the jungle... 'Black Magic Woman,' the song you were dancing to."

This answer appeared to satisfy Julia. She rested her head on his arm and kicked off her sandals.

MTV was showing the Top Ten in the States.

Next came the Top Ten in Britain.

Then in France.

"But... it's the way you dance, too," he added, a little later.

"You think so?" Her voice had a dry edge to it.

"You have something primitive about you... your movements are so—" He had no idea what he wanted to say to her, and left his unfinished sentence hanging in midair over the glass of whiskey. He tried to draw her close to him, but sensed her neck muscles stiffening, as though she was on the point of pulling away. He relaxed the grip of his arm about her shoulders.

A false move. The hero takes his pawn and moves three squares back. A familiar whir of wings was heard, and the mynah landed on the television in front of them.

"Mynah!" Julia said.

"Hi, Maria," said the mynah.

"It talks!" Julia said to Sid, in amazement, and turned back to the mynah. "My name is Ju-li-a," she said, carefully spacing out the syllables.

"Hi, Maria," said the mynah, and hopped onto the table, where it snatched up an empty cigarette carton and shredded it with its beak.

"Ju-li-a," Julia repeated.

She seemed quite absorbed, and Sid edged behind her, taking this opportunity to get in close and squeeze her against him. With his free hand he gently touched the nipple of her left breast. He felt desire surge up inside him, and his legs go weak. Easy, he told himself. Take it easy. It had been so long, he'd been alone month after month. Endless nights in bed with the sound of his bones cracking. He rubbed the nipple between his thumb and first finger. "What are you doing?" Julia asked. Don't move, he said silently. No. Just stay still. But it was already too late. She turned to look at him, and as she turned she rubbed against him. A burning explosion, a blind spurt of fire. Instantaneous. As he came in his pants Sid gave a tiny groan. He snatched his fingers away from her nipple as though they'd been dirtied. "What's the matter with you?" she asked, leaning over him. Sid cleared his throat. "What could be the matter?" he muttered.

"You look—strange."

Another wrong move. The hero collects his dirty laundry and goes back to square one.

"What's your opinion of Brahms?" he asked her.

"Of *Brahms*? What a thing to ask all of a sudden—"

She stared at him in bewilderment.

"You really are a weirdo," she said.

Now I'm going to fuck you, he thought, just keep your mouth shut.

"You make me feel weird," he said, drawing the words out.

They looked at each other without speaking.

The mynah was munching away at the potato chips on the table. Peck, peck, peck. Stupid spoiled bird.

Two hours later Julia, naked, lay idly watching the smoke from her cigarette. Her fingernails were bitten, and Sid wondered how he hadn't noticed this earlier. They'd eaten frozen pizza from the refrigerator. They'd had a spitting competition, targeting first Cher, and then the Spice Girls, on the TV screen. She'd told him that she was studying at some school to become a professional physicians' assistant. And that her mother had died when she was ten. They had made love on the sofa, and he'd seen her sharp little face swallowed up among the cushions, only to reappear pale and beaded with sweat.

"You're much better than you think you are," he told her.

How that came into his head he had no idea.

He watched her frowning, trying to decide whether to take this as a compliment.

"You should become a dancer, you know that?"

"I thought about it once."

"I have some friends who could help you. If you decide to."

Inevitably Sid felt he was falling in love with her.

Inevitably, fatally, in his old familiar cretin way. The same electric discharge from the outer cortex of the brain to the nerve endings of the fingers. At first a numbness in the stomach. And a sense of mild vertigo as he gently touched her shoulders and his hands moved over her, little by little, stroking the down on her arms all the way to her wrists, finally clasping her hands in his and feeling the bitten rims of her nails scraping against his fingers.

The phone rang, and Julia moved aside to make room for him to get up. Sid stayed where he was.

"Aren't you going to answer it?" she asked him.

"It's the Chinese guy," he said.

"Who?"

"A Chinese guy who's trying to sell me a subscription to a paper—" he started to say.

"You're kidding me, right?" she said.

The phone went on ringing.

"Go and see for yourself."

She got up and moved away, tiptoeing barefoot. She was very thin, with a slightly hunched back. From the waist down her figure spread out gently like a pear. He listened to her clipped responses, made in a flat teenage voice, and the click as she replaced the receiver. She walked back to the sofa a little unsteadily. "You were right," she said.

She settled back next to him and put her arms around him.

"I'd like to try out for drama school some time," he heard her say.

"You'll make it, I'm sure," he heard himself tell her.

And he was sure, absolutely.

He brought out the whiskey and they drank it straight from the bottle. "My sister's very sick," he said, "but—" and he was startled to hear his own words traveling through the air, straight to their encounter with Julia—"but I want us to get married."

He saw her home and waited till she unlocked the front door of the apartment building and went inside. Before the elevator door closed behind her, Julia turned and waved to him. A light, friendly gesture. She too seemed glad that things had stopped there. There? Where was that? Sid strolled back to the metro station, zigzag through the bitter-orange trees, and went home.

So?
Everything under control.

"All right," Sid's voice said. "I'll do it for you."
"What?"

Lia was standing in the corridor talking on the public phone.

"That nurse," Sid said. "I'll do what you asked me to. I need to know his name."

Lia remained silent. At the other end of the line Sid heard her breathe out gently, as though she was trying to think.

Finally she said: "It's not on now."
"Why not?"

"Because it isn't." Her voice sounded nervous and exhausted.

"All right, then—"

"Wait," she said.

"What?"

"Don't hang up."

Sid waited, cleaning out the mynah bird's cage. He didn't want his impatience to show.

"I had this dream—" Lia said, and broke off.

Sid went on waiting without showing any sign of impatience. He was now emptying the mynah's tray and cups.

"I had this dream—"

"And?"

"I saw you and Sharon Stone together. You were at the Hilton and I'd come to meet you there. You hardly opened your mouth, but she was very friendly. I lied to her, said I'd been to the Oscar awards ceremony. She didn't seem impressed. 'We were away then,' she told me, and smiled, showing her wonderful teeth. 'We'd come to Greece.' To Greece, I thought, and you never said a word to me? I felt my heart stop, the way it does in dreams, you know? I was ready to burst into tears but I didn't want you to notice. Still, the worst part was still to come. Get this, now. I was really distraught and on the point of leaving. I collected my cape from the cloakroom, and then the scene changed to some kind of lounge in the hotel, and I walked out. With my heart broken, like I said. As I was going along the corridor with my cape over my arm, a walking stick popped out of it, followed by a red scarf. Any moment now they'll be followed by a rabbit, I thought, and instantly realized what had happened. At the coat-check they'd given me the magician's cape instead of mine. I had to take it back—"

"Incredible. And how was—"

"What? The cape?"

"No, Sharon Stone."

"Like Sharon Stone. But—now that I think of it—what really strikes me is something quite different. Why didn't I use the magician's cape to scare you, get back at you? Because really deep down that was a betrayal, wasn't it?"

"I don't know..." He tried to consider the idea, but needed more time. Now he just felt disoriented.

"I have to hang up," Lia said suddenly. "There's a line."

"A line?"

"Waiting to use the phone."

It was visiting hours. Lia had not the slightest urge to go back to the ward. The new patient was getting on her nerves. She had arrived two days earlier, and today she was expecting visitors. She had announced this to Lia with an irritated air, as though she was doing her relatives a favor by letting them come and see her in hospital.

The woman looked absolutely exhausted. Her face was drawn, and there were dark rings etched under her eyes. She was telling them how sick she was, going on about how for the past eight years every germ in existence had hit her, how she'd caught a whole array of diseases, one after the other, without ever getting well. Not for one day, one hour even, had she stopped suffering. Her relatives listened to her with barely controlled impatience. They had made the trip from Larisa to see her, driving 200 miles or so through the heat in an ancient Toyota, and now they seemed to be wondering why they'd come.

A plump woman, wearing a green dress with thin shoulder straps, was sitting at the foot of the bed, fanning herself with a crumpled magazine. "It's hot," the patient said, as though her mind was on something else, and began describing the symptoms of Malta fever. The woman in the green dress turned and looked at the two men silently leaning on the bed rails. The younger one kept running his hand through his hair.

"I could do with something to cool me off," the woman said, sighing.

"Sorry, sorry," the patient whined, "I haven't offered you anything, I'm really losing my mind—"

"Don't get up, I'll go," Lia offered, anxious not to miss this chance to escape from the ward. She sprang out of bed and started off, pulling her I.V. stand behind her. The older man followed her. She'd hoped that the woman in the green dress would have come out with her—they could have started a conversation in the corridor.

The kitchen was a bare room with two sinks and a large refrigerator. The refrigerator was for the patients. Each of them had her own place on one of the shelves and marked it off, as the fancy took her, with an apple, a paper napkin, or even by spreading out a magazine cover. But there were often squabbles. When the hospital was full, when all the beds were occupied. The oldest patients, the fixtures, would often take over more space, an inch today, two tomorrow. Lia's corner spot on the third rack was usually empty because she never bought anything, so that the others had little by little encroached on her space. Now she took the bottle of orangeade out of the refrigerator and looked around for plastic glasses.

"Where are they?" she said to herself. The man was standing in the middle of the kitchen watching her. "Where are they?" she said again. She was beginning to get irritated with herself for having taken the initiative. The sink was full of unwashed glasses. She went over, chose five that looked not quite as dirty as the rest, turned on the faucet and began washing them.

"They told us she was at death's door," said the elderly man, from behind her shoulder.

"I wouldn't know," Lia mumbled. She took the bottle from the counter and began carefully filling the glasses. Would there, she wondered, be enough orangeade for everyone?

"She looks just great to me," the man went on. He was hovering over her as though waiting to hear something further. "In fine shape," he added, with a little sigh.

"I can only carry one glass," Lia said, pointing to her I.V. stand.

"That's OK," the man assured her, "I'll come back for them."

Back in the ward no one was talking. The woman in green was standing by the window, looking sulky, and the younger man had wandered over to Lia's bedside and was leafing through the books on her nightstand. The sick woman, an exhausted smile on her face, was staring straight ahead at nothing in particular. "Excuse me—just curiosity," the man said as he saw them come in, and put the book down. "No problem," said Lia. She sat down on the bed. If Sid had been there, she thought, they could have gotten a laugh out of the situation. The older man went back to the kitchen and returned with the rest of the glasses. The patient drained hers in greedy gulps and then let her head drop back on the pillow. "You might just as well have poisoned me," she sighed.

Yet five minutes later she sat up in bed, asked them to stack the pillows behind her back, and was talking away with much animated gesturing. Doctors don't know a thing, that was her theme, doctors are no help, all they understand is how to make you sick. I'm a better doctor than they are. I can prove it. Her eyes glinted. "You," she said, addressing the older man, "tell me what complaints you have." He looked at her, startled. "I don't really—" he began. "No, come on, tell me," she interrupted him. "and I'll make you better!" She thumped her chest. The older man glanced uneasily at the other two, who were listening to this exchange as though it had nothing to do with them. Finally he said: "I have high blood pressure... due to nerves."

"Right," the patient announced triumphantly, "I'll tell you what to do: never visit a doctor, never set foot inside a hospital! You hear me?"

A nurse came in to tell them that visiting hours were over. The woman in green went to the bathroom to freshen up and came back hurriedly, waving her hands in the air. "There's no towel," she said. They all collected their things, and each in turn approached the patient's bedside to say goodbye to her. They were at the door on their way out when she raised her head in their direction and shouted: "I want to die—don't go!"

"You should have seen their expressions. Like scalded mice."

"And what did they do?"

"Nothing. Just goggled at her. Only the young one went back to her and said: 'Come on, Auntie, you're going to see us all buried.' But she acted like she didn't hear him, and screamed again, as loud as she could, 'I want to die.' "

Sid had come by to see her the next day, bringing the Sunday papers. It was early evening, when visits to the ward were not allowed, so they sat out in the courtyard.

"Last time I was here, there were these two old guys sitting on the bench, you just wouldn't believe it—"

"What's so extraordinary about two old guys?"

"You think I'm kidding? One of them was trying to push shares to the other—"

Lia giggled. "And that impressed you?"

"Two wacky old farts talking investments? One of them with no teeth, and the other hooked up to a urine bag?"

"But what was it that impressed you?"

"You know what I mean."

"Yes, I know, whereas you just think you know."

"OK then."

"So, what are we going to do about the Prize Student?"

"Who?" Sid stared at her, disconcerted.

"The nurse."

"I await your instructions."

"He mustn't run into you here."

"Just let me know when he's on duty, then."

"Right. What are you planning to do?"

"Leave that to me."

· 5 ·

*T*he one thing that got on Sotiris's nerves was the telephone. He liked peace and quiet, the assurance that no one was going to bother him in his own home. He lived in a studio apartment. By himself. Who was going to call him nowadays? Basically no one: just his mother, every Saturday that he wasn't on duty in the hospital, and the occasional distant relative passing through Athens. Until the appearance on the scene of Thanási, this old classmate of his, who'd called and wanted to see him. They arranged a meeting at a patisserie two blocks away from his house. After a couple of beers Thanási got out his money to pay. "Ah," he said with a sigh, "I could do with one of those Corfiote ginger beers we used to drink." He collected his change and left a generous tip for the waiter. Sotiris, who didn't recall ever having had such a classmate, and on top of that had never been to Corfu, sighed too, out of politeness. Thanási's face didn't stir any memories. Still, he told himself, it was years ago, we've all changed, I've just got to be patient.

All the same, he had to admit that Thanási was over-sentimental. At one point a tear rolled down his cheek, and he quickly wiped it away, pretending that he'd been overcome by a fit of coughing. A deliberate move so that Sotiris wouldn't notice. But Sotiris saw it. Even so, the shared memories this old friend was digging up didn't ring a bell with him at all. "Remember the crib sheet of Mendeléyev's Periodic Table you passed me during the chemistry exam? You really saved me that time!" And then, right after that, voice trembling with emotion, Thanási had gone on: "Remember that school trip when you made me smoke, and I coughed and my eyes kept watering and I couldn't inhale the smoke and you blew your top and told me that if I didn't do it I'd never get to be a man?" He must be off his rocker, Sotiris thought, and suddenly found himself longing for his nice little apartment, all quiet and clean and there ready for him, with artichokes à la Polita in the fridge. But the fact that in all these stories he figured as the strong guy, while Thanási was the weakling, and more often than not the victim, had made a big impression on him.

"You always had such a personality!" Thanási sighed at one stage. What's all this about? Sotiris wondered. He began to feel uneasy. Could he be working up to hit me for a loan? But Thanási, as though divining his fears, began a new spiel, saying that anything he needed, money, women even—he added, lowering his voice—if he wanted someone roughed up, he, Thanási, was there. "Anything," he emphasized, with a wink. Sotiris listened to him without speaking. He'd made up his mind to stay quiet and friendly to the end, and besides, at the back of his mind he had those artichokes waiting for him, sweet with just the right dash of tartness to them. He'd brought them back from the village in a Tupperware, figuring that they'd last three days. And when he got back home, and sat down to eat in front of the television, he began to mull over the various phases of his encounter with Thanási, slowly chewing his food and dipping big hunks of bread in the sauce. The bottom line was, he hadn't lost anything. He'd got out for a bit, and on top of that his friend had picked up the tab. A little company did him good. By the time he'd sorted out all these ideas and begun to watch the program on TV, he saw that the jar was empty. His old classmate had given him an appetite.

The next day Thanási called twice, asking if there was anything he needed, if he was feeling all right, if he'd slept well the night before, etc. Sotiris thought it might not be a bad idea to meet him again, but waited for Thanási to make the first move. "You don't get enough sleep," Thanási said, "I thought you looked dead tired," and hung up. Sotiris switched on the television and spent the rest of the evening wondering whether Thanási would call again. But the phone didn't ring. At ten o'clock he set his alarm clock for six a.m. and went to sleep. Maybe Thanási was right. He really tired himself out at the hospital. He should get more sleep.

At seven-thirty precisely the following evening the phone rang. Sotiris let it ring three, four, five times before he picked up the receiver, savoring in advance the conversation that would follow.

"Are you all right?" Thanási's voice at the other end of the line sounded worried.

Sotiris gave a vague answer about doing hospital accounts, or some such thing.

"All work and no play makes Jack a dull boy," Thanási said. He paused a moment, then added: "I was afraid something might have happened to you."

What could happen? Sotiris wondered as he looked around. Television, fridge, the little gas burner with its coffee pot—everything was in its place.

"I've got my eye on this great little place," Thanási was saying, and began to describe the appetizers, the retsina, the view of the Acropolis, and, above all, the cleanness of the place. "Just like your mother's home cooking," he went on. "Because I know how fussy you are, how hard to please—" He left it at that.

They sat at a table outside the taverna, under an old plane tree. There was a small open space by the roadside, with two dried-up flower beds and a statue on a plinth between them. Sotiris heard the noise of cats hunting through garbage.

"Can you imagine it," Thanási began when their wine arrived, "all that up there existing two, two-and-a-half millennia ago, and here we are now—"

Sotiris followed his gaze and saw a section of level rock lit up by searchlights. Its summit resembled a flattened platform. At its foot houses sprouted unevenly, like teeth.

"And here we sit still today, spending our time on—bullshit." For a moment Thanási seemed really angry. "Well, cheers," he said, and raised his glass.

"Cheers." Sotiris didn't like seeing his school friend irritated.

"It's a good thing you're around," he heard him say then, in a milder voice.

Sotiris nodded. A waiter was coming out of the taverna in their direction, with a loaded tray.

Thanási had ordered half the menu: a country salad, split-pea purée, braised veal, fried anchovies and squid. Sotiris loved squid. Even if they'd been splitting the bill all this would have made it worthwhile. Splitting the bill? He felt a twinge of anxiety. But his friend had invited him, no two ways about that.

A cat emerged from the open lot and slowly sidled across to them, its tail up like a flagpole. A tiger with yellow eyes. If it comes under the table I'll kick it, Sotiris thought.

"Let's not beat about the bush," Thanási said, and put his fork down on his plate. Sotiris stared at him distractedly, feeling the mouthful of bread and split-pea purée melt in his mouth, spreading its sweetness over his palate.

"No, I mean—only if you want to, that is—let's be straight." He'd started getting that wild look in his eye again.

"OK, fine," Sotiris muttered, swallowing.

"Like in the old days. Man-to-man stuff. If you want to," Thanási insisted.

"OK," Sotiris said again, and waited. He now had a gristly chunk of squid in his mouth.

"Well," said Thanási, staring at the dishes on the table, as though they were the cause of his irritation, "you're going to waste in that hospital."

Sotiris remained silent.

"Going to waste, d'you hear me?"

"Hmmm," Sotiris said, taking on the expression of someone carefully considering what he has heard. A fragment of squid had got stuck in one of his molars, and nothing he tried could get it out.

"You seem thoughtful," Thanasi said.

"I'm listening," said Sotiris. He considered putting a finger in his mouth, but Thanási would notice.

"Yes," Thanási went on, "you listen." He emphasized the word. "You know how to listen, that's your great talent. That's how you were back in school. Sotiris the philosopher, that's what the teachers called you, remember?"

Another detail that had escaped his mind. When had that happened? How many years ago? But he had no intention of letting memories bother him tonight, so he just looked at Thanási, waiting for him to go on.

"I know very well the heavy responsibilities you have in that hospital," Thanási sighed. "Demands by the doctors, the patients and their whims—just thinking about it sends the blood to my head. Someone with your personality!"

Sotiris reflected on the struggle he'd had to get his hospital job. His parents were still sending a big can of olive oil annually to the politician who'd put in a word for him. But he decided to say nothing about this.

"And now I'm sitting with you here, right here under all these marble monuments," his old classmate went on, voice shaking with emotion, "in the shadow of the sacred rock!"

Sotiris cast a bored eye in the rock's direction. From where he was sitting he could discern a bare flagstaff, and beyond it two broken columns wilting in the orange glare of the spotlights. The entire rock was walled off. Right outside the walls was a tumbledown house, in the act of yawning.

"What's your job?" he asked Thanási, to change the subject.

"Mine?" Thanási repeated, surprised. He looked up at the rock again with a dreamy expression, and said, softly, "What you always were telling me to get into—business."

Sotiris had kicked off his shoes under the table. He felt the cat's soft fur against the arch of his sole, and shivered. With his forefinger he caressed it gently on the nape of its neck. The cat didn't move. Under its pelt he sensed an inner stirring, the beginning of a purr. Now it's going to scratch me, he thought. He carefully withdrew his foot.

"The things the Parthenon and all those monuments teach us—" Thanási was off again. "You said it first, remember? 'The one thing I know is that I know nothing.' "

Sotiris felt around with his toes for his shoe, located it, and got it back on.

"Listen, kid, you used to tell me: *The one thing I know is that I know nothing.* Make sure you remember that. I never forgot it. I swear to you."

People were leaving. One after another, the tables had begun to empty. Sotiris got his other shoe on, and was working up to giving the cat a kick, but at the critical moment it went and curled up at the far end of the table. Now he couldn't reach it even if he stretched his leg right out. Filthy female. He tried to focus his attention on what Thanási was saying: he was still chattering away, but looked a bit tired. Sotiris stared at the food left on the plates. Then he saw the cat slip out from under the table and move off, slowly and nonchalantly.

· 6 ·

*T*here was a boy in Nina's life, but no one knew it. In the evenings, she would whisper his name as she stroked the balcony railing, her back turned to the others. Way off in front of her, willows drooped in the moonlight, their shivering leaves forming silvery webs, and she could hear the distant hollow surge of waves washing in over clumps of wrack. Without making a sound, Nina would say his name again and again. Her lips half-parted, she would roll its first two consonants on the tip of her tongue, letting the rest of it flow out freely, filling her mouth with a taste of strawberry ice cream.

Behind her, the customers were playing pinochle, backgammon, gin rummy. The sound of laughter and good-humored banter spread through the air along with the chirr of the cicadas. Every so often someone would get up and ask her to empty the ashtrays or bring some iced beers. I love you, I love you, she'd say to herself as she left her place at the darkest corner of the balcony to go get the beers from the refrigerator, which was inside the coffeeshop just before the kitchen. I love you. The fridge was crammed with watermelon halves, and dripped. Nina knelt in a puddle of sugary juice, and Blackie scampered across to her and rubbed against her legs. "I love you, I love you," she told him, caressing his damp muzzle.

"Nina! *Nina!* Where are you?"

"Just coming—"

That was how it went on all summer, and no one, not even her sister, suspected a thing. The boy's name was Stephanos, and he'd come with his parents to spend the summer in the village. He was the best-looking kid in the world, with fair hair, freckles, and New Balance shoes. His shoelaces were always untied. His parents would walk on ahead, while he always kept behind, as if careful to emphasize the distance that separated him from them, as if he regarded them with a touch of contempt. "Stephanos, Stephanos!" his mother would call out when they got to the beach. That was how Nina had found out his name. His mother, feet in the hot sand, would be waiting for him to come and help put up the beach umbrella. "Stephanos!" Then he'd stroll across to her, in no kind of hurry, as if he were seeing her for the first time.

"Nina! Where on earth have you got to? What are you doing?"

"Just coming—"

A noise from the back part of the house caught her attention. Beyond the kitchen were the storeroom and the toilet, and behind them the garden. She heard a thud, and the sound of something breaking. Then silence. As she stood there motionless, holding the beers, ears alert, a muffled voice said "Fuck it," and Blackie sat up on his haunches and barked. There came the sound of the toilet flushing, and Mr. Papazoglou appeared from the far side of the kitchen and stood there in front of her, perspiring heavily. He was a retired doctor, spending his summer in the house next door. Nina had gone there once, when Aunt Lela fainted. He looked out of breath, his shirt was half unbuttoned, and when he saw her startled expression he burst out laughing. "Who was the father of Zebedee's children?"* he asked, and without stopping for an answer brushed past her and went out.

"The beers, Nina!" someone shouted from the balcony. She bent down, gave the puppy one last pat, and hurried off.

Her sister was standing beside one group, adding up their bill. She tore the sheet off the pad and left it on the table.

"Zoe," said Nina, as she came up to her, "let's go for a walk, shall we?" To the waterfront, to the old harbor. To the van beside which the gypsy laid out his watermelons in the road, holding up the traffic. Sometimes Stephanos and his parents would go that way late in the evening, on their way home from the restaurant.

*A nonsense question that grown-ups used to put to children. *Trans.*

"Zoe's got work to do, can't you see?" said Aunt Lela, in a frantic rush from the kitchen. Aunt Lela was their father's sister, and a widow. She had sliced up a big cucumber, stuck toothpicks in the slices, and was busy setting up appetizers to go with the ouzo.

"Later, then? Can we go later?" Nina persisted.

"That's too late," Aunt Lela said.

"I'm not going anywhere with her," Zoe said. "The last time she walked me off my feet—we went all the way to the old harbor, and even then she wouldn't stay put."

"The old harbor? What on earth did you go there for?" Aunt Lela asked.

"I don't know—she told me she wanted to look at Mt. Paliovouna, that you can see it better from there," Zoe said.

"Bravo, an interest in geography," commented Mr. Papazoglou. He was standing at the bar, opposite Aunt Lela, putting water in his ouzo.

"There was some guy hiding at the old harbor and watching us," Nina said, and instantly regretted having spoken. She too had now come over to the counter.

"Who was watching you?" Aunt Lela asked Zoe. "What actually happened?"

"I haven't a clue. I didn't see a thing," Zoe said casually. She began to clear the table of a group that had just left.

"That's a lie!" Nina exclaimed.

"I didn't see anything," Zoe repeated in a quiet voice, and went on with her work.

"There was someone there, for a long time,

watching us, he left cigarette butts everywhere, you saw them too, and you saw the way the oleanders had been crushed where he'd been sitting," said Nina, without drawing breath.

"Give me a drop more ouzo," said Mr. Papazoglou. Aunt Lela poured him some, and stood there looking thoughtful. Zoe picked up her trayful of dirty glasses and went into the kitchen.

No one paid attention to her any more. Oh Stephanos, Stephanos, where are you? Nina wondered. There was no one in this dump who loved her. She'd have done better to stay with her parents, even if that meant no swimming. No swimming ever again. Never again to set eyes on the sea.

"Nina," said Aunt Lela, "why don't you go inside and watch television?"

"Don't want to," she said, but she got up and went.

Nobody loves me. Stephanos, Stephanos! I'd be better off dead than listening to their stupid chatter. Then they'll all cry and be sorry for the way they treated me, and Zoe'll lie there kicking and screaming the way she did when that car ran over Blackie's mom, but it'll be too late. She'll never get over her grief. Never. That last "never" made her feel somewhat better, and she stood there in the dark for a little, thinking. It was very hot. Every five minutes the fridge would snort as though about to expire, fall silent, and then suddenly start its rumbling again. I love you, Nina said to herself. I'll love you for the rest of my life. But suppose he asked her to give up everything for his sake? Suppose he demanded something terrible and perverse of her, like strangling

Blackie with her own two hands? But he's not going to ask me for anything. I know he isn't. Ever. He's not going to ask me for anything because he doesn't love me. He hasn't even noticed me. Doesn't even know who I am. And why should he notice me? I haven't got breasts, I don't know how to kiss... From the balcony came the sound of whispering. Mr. Papazoglou guffawed. "Don't, please don't," Aunt Lela kept repeating. Then she too burst into crazy laughter, as though she was choking.

"I love you," Nina said, and hugged the refrigerator. It was just about her height. It gave a tiny shuddering groan, and fell silent again. She held her breath too. "I love you," she repeated, caressing its cold surface. The knife used for cutting up the watermelons was hanging there on its hook. In the darkness she found and grasped its handle. Then she slowly slid her fingers along the blade. They'll all be sorry, she thought. "You'll be sorry," she whispered. She heard a light patter of approaching feet. "Blackie," she murmured. She knelt down in front of the refrigerator door. "Blackie, come here to me."

She put one arm round the puppy's neck and hugged it close to her. With her free hand she took the knife and scratched a cross on her knee. I swear eternal love to you, she said silently. The puppy was panting quickly, impatient to be off. "That's how it is, Blackie," she said. "You've got to learn." Then she licked the blade clean and put the knife back in its place.

· 7 ·

*A*wful weather. Dry. Parched. And a white, stony sun. In the ward not a breath stirring, everything still, the very air clinging sluggishly to itself.

"I shouldn't have drunk that milk," said the sick woman. "I knew it, I didn't want to drink it, I told them, don't give me milk, I said, I can't handle it— And then I drank it. For two days I was all right. Well, sort of all right, that is. Borderline all right, certainly not the frightful state I'm in now. Now and again everything would go dark, I'd lose my vision. It's nothing, they told me, just your nerves, it'll go away. Nerves? Me? I was the one who sat quiet as a lamb in my chair when I stayed up all night watching over my dead mother. And when the Germans were bombing us I was the one who kept singing away like a lark in the shelter. So the third day, they took me to the doctor, they couldn't stand me any more. It's natural at your age, he said, and pocketed a 10,000-drachma note without giving me a receipt. Just menopause, said the murderer. You hear that? I wasn't even thirty-five, everyone took me for a young girl. But the best of it came later, it was then my real agony started. And that murderer is going around out there a free man, you hear me? A free man, while I'm stuck on this bed with one foot in the grave..."

Her voice gradually faded, and it looked as though she'd fallen asleep. Lia took a sip of tea and tried to concentrate on the book she was reading.

"I shouldn't have drunk that milk," the sick woman began again, "that's how I picked up Malta fever, and then all the rest followed—dizzy spells, bile, asthma, a whole host of troubles—" She broke off here, and stared up at the ceiling.

It was almost time for the doctors' rounds. Nurses hurried from ward to ward, having one last look round to make sure everything was in order. The Professor was very punctilious. His station had to be a model of perfection. A roll of toilet paper left by a washbasin, or a packet of crackers on a patient's nightstand, could drive him frantic. Lia smiled to herself. She was very fond of him. He was a little man of about sixty, thin and nervous, with pink skin and well-cared-for hands—Uh-oh! The Prize Student had come into the ward, and was eyeing her with the air of an inspector-general.

"And how are we today?" he asked.

The idiot's started talking like Kalotychos, Lia thought.

"How d'you think?" sighed the sick woman.

"The sun's shining, the birds are singing," Lia murmured.

"What was that?" the nurse said, and took a step in the direction of her bed.

"Everything's fine," said Lia.

The nurse moved to the doorway, stuck his head through it, and looked around impatiently. Voices became audible from the corridor outside. "They're coming! They're coming!" he exclaimed, turning round. Then he stood to attention and waited.

The business of doctors' rounds always had the air of a ceremony, even though it took place daily. First there was a hum of voices as the doctors approached the ward. A sudden hum amid absolute silence. Then the Professor would lead the way into the ward, briskly, without looking at anyone. By his side, but at the same time half a step behind him, precisely coordinated, came his two assistants with the patients' files. And trotting along behind them the rest of the crowd, a cluster of doctors, nurses, and students.

"How are we today?" Kalotychos had gone straight over to the sick woman's bed. One of his assistants was holding her file open in front of him. The other was bringing him her temperature chart. Behind them the students were opening their pads to take notes.

Lia watched the Prize Student. He was standing apart from the group, cockily, watching the activity. But he wasn't listening to a word of it, of that she was certain. His mind was on something quite different. Something that was giving him complete satisfaction. Sid hadn't called. Lia wondered whether her brother had already put some plan into action. But if he had he'd have let me know, she thought. Unless he wants to surprise me.

"Don't let me hear such nonsense," Kalotychos was saying. "With Sjogren's Disease there are no lachrymatory symptoms—" One of his assistants leaned down and whispered something in his ear. He shook his head.

"Sjogren?" the sick woman raised her head. "What have I got now, doctor?"

The Professor took no notice of her. "You mustn't depend on symptoms alone," he said, turning to the students, who hung on his words, pens raised. "Symptoms can very often lead us astray."

Professor Kalotychos.

The terror of the medical school.

He cheered her up every time. Even on her worst days.

Her turn had now come. She sat up in bed and smiled.

"Well?" Kalotychos said, smiling back at her.

"The same."

"Let's see where we stand, then," he said. His assistant held out her file, and he took it. He leafed through it in silence for a little, nervously tapping one finger against the cover. Then he turned round. "Well, gentlemen—and ladies," he added, as he caught sight of a female student at the back, her face pitted with acne. He carefully made eye contact with each one of them before addressing his topic.

"This case would appear to be—" Behind the row of heads Lia saw the Prize Student snap into focus and listen with careful attention.

"I told them about the gout but they didn't listen," the sick woman complained as soon as the doctors had gone. "My feet are swollen, I can't wear shoes, but I might as well be talking to the stone-deaf... it's the gout, that's what started it all—"

"I thought it all started with the Malta fever," Lia broke in.

"Yes of course, it was the Malta fever, but there was this gout too—" The sick woman clearly wasn't going to be intimidated.

She was the worst roommate Lia had had in the whole six months. Lia got up, took her I.V. stand, and left the ward. At the far end of the corridor there was a small roof terrace, where visitors went when they wanted a cigarette. She opened the French windows and stepped out. It was a dull, dry day. The horizon was nowhere visible: in every direction the city sprawled out interminably. Lia stared into the distance at the gray buildings, the criss-cross of roads, the cardboard homes stacked heavily on top of each other under a layer of rusty smog. Each neighborhood merged into the next, suffocating it. From up there the city looked half-finished. As though it had never been completed, and yet had already started to fall apart, to turn into ruins. Suddenly she felt nostalgia: a wave of harsh nostalgia for the life down there, inside those gray apartment blocks, those wretched cramped apartments where the neighbors' quarrels came straight through the thin rickety walls, penetrated your room, skewered your heart. A wild hunger seized her: for day-to-day life and its problems, for a boring ordinary life. If she could only find herself there just for one single day. In a grimy efficiency, down in the basement of one of those apartment blocks. To spend even one afternoon there. To sip her coffee slowly, standing by the slit of a window, staring out. To discern, in the remote distance, on some forgotten and unreal planet, this very roof terrace, Ward 11, the hospital. "I don't want to stay here any longer," she said aloud. Amid the stillness of the scene the echo of her voice came winging back, was trapped inside her. I don't want to! I don't want to! Her eyes filled with tears.

Sotiris was sitting in the head nurse's office. His shift didn't end till six, and it was still only three. He had no idea how to kill time. He had cleaned the thermometers with alcohol, and returned them to their proper place. He had collected the bedpans and taken them to the bathroom. He had counted out the pills for each patient's evening dose and put them in little envelopes marked with the right ward number and bed number. Now he was waiting. Thanási had called him the night before, saying he had to see him, it was urgent. That there was a problem. Sotiris had hoped for an evening at the taverna, but Thanási had insisted on meeting him at his place. He'd emphasized that it was something very serious. Still, Sotiris wasn't worried.

By now he'd got used to his old classmate's exaggerated emotions. He must have remembered something else, Sotiris thought, another episode from the old days. Could I have saved his life at some point? Maybe he was in danger of drowning on some school trip, and I rescued him? At great risk to my own life? The idea was far-fetched, but one could expect anything from Thanási. Anyhow, Sotiris had no complaints. Three times now they'd gone out, and every time his old classmate had picked up the tab. Even the ringing of the phone, which once sent him into a nervous tizzy, was now becoming routine. Before he'd jump up at the first trill, as if he'd been jabbed with a needle, but not any more. He knew it was Thanási, and Thanási always came up with some pleasant suggestion. He began to recall the food on the taverna table, the split-pea purée, the veal, the deep-fried squid—mmm, that squid! He was beginning to feel hungry. He decided to go down to the kitchen in the basement. If the cook hadn't left she would give him something.

The corridor was deserted. Everything was quiet, the doors to the wards closed. The patients would be asleep. How long would he be away from his post? It would take him ten minutes, a quarter of an hour at most, to go downstairs, find the cook and hurry back again. Their unit was on the fifth floor. The elevator was out of order. But even when it wasn't he preferred using the stairs. No danger that way of running into someone like Kalotychos. And the stairs led straight down to the basement, right by the kitchens.

As he went down the steps, he couldn't help casting a quick glance at the other units, and smirking in satisfaction. Crowds, confusion, hubbub. He could never work in such conditions. Nobody observed visiting hours there. Gurneys were left around in the corridors, and the patients traipsed up and down like zombies, clutching their nylon bags. His unit by comparison was a tomb. The Professor wanted it in apple-pie order: he was a fierce watchdog, but he had a point. There was no one down in the kitchens. The heat inside was overwhelming, and thick with various smells. The women must have slipped out into the courtyard to take a break. He opened the oven and saw a pan with roasted potatoes in it, picked out the brownest and ate them with his fingers. He also found a hunk of bread, and took two more potatoes. Then he shut the oven and left.

The corridor of his unit was bathed in light. All was quiet, exactly as he had left it. But his hands were sticky with oil, and that annoyed him. The bathroom for the hospital staff was next to the physicians' office. He soaped his hands twice, rinsed them, then held them under the drier. He actually wasn't bad-looking, he thought, staring at himself in the mirror. Regular features, a straight nose. Why, you might even stretch a point and call him handsome. If only he didn't wear glasses. If only his ears didn't stick out. His mother told him they gave him a smart appearance, pricked up like a dog's when it scents danger and is trying to determine where it's coming from. Hmmm—the dog slowly turns its head, ears cocked, and picks up the enemy's scent from far off. And then it barks. Woof. Maybe Mama Koula was right.

As he came out of the bathroom he heard a noise in the physicians' office. Who could it be? The head nurse had left earlier. There were no other nurses about—he was the only one on duty. He listened again. Someone was definitely in there. He took a deep breath and silently opened the door. At first he couldn't make out who it was. He saw a white figure kneeling on the floor, bent over some open files. All the doctors' files had been pulled off the shelves and now lay scattered over the floor.

"What's going on here?"

The figure turned its head. He should have guessed. It was that halfwitted girl from Ward 11.

"I wanted to see my file," she said, not in the least disconcerted, turned away again, and went on with her reading.

"That's against the rules!"

He was a quiet fellow, what could he do? This is what he was thinking as he left the hospital after his shift. As he threaded his way through the bitter-orange trees. A quiet fellow, no outbursts of temper, that was the picture he had of himself. No extreme moods. So long as no one provoked him. So long as no one really stepped on his toes. Leave sheep to shepherds, his father got that one right. Everyone should stick to his own job. There are rules, and this halfwitted girl had really crossed the line. From the first moment he saw her he knew something bad was going to happen. Right from the start she'd stood out, like a fly in the milk pail. And now because of her he was so upset he was shaking. While he stood waiting for the bus he ran over that afternoon's events in his mind. He'd found her in the physicians' office. He'd caught her red-handed, opening files and reading them. He'd told her this was forbidden, he'd shouted it at her again and again. She had simply ignored him, and kept on reading as if nothing was happening. He'd gone up to her and snatched at the file in her hands. She wouldn't let go, but clung to it like a madwoman. Then he shoved her. What else could he do? Yet not even then would she give up the file. She'd stared at him with a strange weasel-like expression. With contempt: that was how she'd looked at him. It was then that he'd hit her. Once, smack on the jaw, so hard that her face flipped. She dropped the file then. Got to her feet, very slowly, and went out of the room.

He stayed there in all the mess, waiting for a senior nurse from some other unit to show up, for Professor Kalotychos to come bursting in, beside himself with fury. While he waited, he began to tidy things up. Not a sound. Absolutely quiet. No crying or shouting. He went out into the corridor, expecting to find her at the public phone, as he'd done on other occasions, but she wasn't there. What could he do? He went to the head nurse's office and waited. When the staff nurse arrived for the next shift, he collected his things to leave. In the corridor he stopped outside Ward 11, opened the door, and peered inside. She was lying there with her face to the wall. Quite still. He closed the door and left.

· 8 ·

*H*ello there, old buddy." Thanási was standing outside Sotiris's door with a cage in his hand.

Inside the cage was a large black bird.

Black as pitch, with a yellow beak.

"Aren't you going to ask me in?"

Sotiris retreated.

Thanási put the cage down beside the television. It was almost a yard high, with a couple of water troughs, a yellow tube like a chute, and a swing. A bird swing. They sat down, Thanási in the only armchair, and Sotiris on a plain seat. Thanási lit a cigarette and looked around him.

"Nice little place you've got here."

"A bachelor's bits and pieces."

"Yeah, still—" Thanási sighed, and fell silent,

staring at the ash on his cigarette. Sotiris put an ashtray in front of him. What next? he wondered. His old classmate looked worried sick. But what about the bird? How did the bird fit in? It huddled there on the floor of its cage as though asleep, but it wasn't missing a thing: its eyes kept swiveling left and right as though by clockwork. Ugly bitch of a bird, Sotiris thought. It occurred to him that he'd take great pleasure in wringing its neck. No, better still, tossing it into a pot of boiling water, and seeing how those mean, disgusting eyes looked at him then.

"This is my daughter, Maria," Thanási said, nodding toward the cage.

Sotiris laughed, a laugh with no smile.

"I mean it," Thanási said. "Seriously." He knelt in front of the cage and blew cigarette smoke into it. "Come here, kiddo." The bird blinked its eyes and didn't budge. Thanási sat down in the armchair again.

"It's a long story," he began. The cigarette had burned right down to his fingers. "It goes back to the time when I lost touch with you—when we finished school, I mean. All my life I've been struggling, battling on my own—no wife, no friends—with only one purpose—'The one thing I know is that I know nothing.' Remember how we told each other that under the Acropolis?"

Sotiris quietly took the cigarette butt from his old classmate's fingers and stubbed it out in the ashtray. Thanási didn't seem to notice.

"All these tough years this bird is the only company I've had. The only one who stood by me, gave me courage when I was ready to fold, so that

I'd get on my feet again, move forward, keep going. So that I became the man I am today." Thanási looked himself up and down.

"Fine, um, how old is it, then?" Sotiris asked, eager to cut this discussion short.

"How old's what?"

"The bird, of course, what's its age?"

"It's ten—I've had it ever since the year after we left school. A real little miss," he added, with an affectionate smile.

"I had no idea they lived that long."

A kind of nervous itch had begun to affect Sotiris. And in his heart of hearts he was disappointed, he knew that. He'd spent the entire day impatiently waiting for Thanási's visit. Especially after the episode at the hospital. Today he might even have talked to him, told him all about it. Everything, the whole business of that halfwit. How he'd caught her red-handed, how she'd reacted, how she'd been behaving toward him from the first moment she set foot in the hospital. And how he'd hit her, a really nasty wallop that might have hurt her, might even have done her some lasting damage. And that now he might lose his job. He'd been waiting for his old classmate to come and cheer him up. But for the past half-hour he'd been sitting there opposite him as he went on and on about a bird. Singing its praises quite extravagantly, too.

"You're my best friend," Thanási was saying. "My only friend, actually." He paused for a moment. "I want to ask a favor of you. I know you won't refuse me, you're the only person I could ask to do something like this—"

Sotiris eyed the bird. It was still roosting, but it looked all set to pounce. Its eyes were bugging out of their sockets. Then he heard Thanási saying that he had to go away on business for a few days, that Sotiris was the only person he could entrust his bird to, that only knowing it was with him he would feel relaxed and not worry, that the bird had a really affectionate nature, it was just a bit coquettish, and, finally, that he was sure Sotiris would, in three days or so, become so fond of it—"so attached to it" were his exact words—that he wouldn't want to give it back again.

The rest happened very fast. Thanási presented him with a box of birdseed, quickly explained how to clean the cage and change the water, leaned down and blew the bird a kiss, at which it didn't bat an eyelid, thanked Sotiris, and shot off.

I didn't manage to get a word out, Sotiris thought later. I didn't even have a chance to tell him I have to go out of town back to the village, and how the hell can I travel with that bird? How did I get caught up in this mess? He was sitting in the armchair opposite the birdcage, exactly where Thanási had been sitting earlier. He began thinking back over the sequence of events at the hospital, in the order in which they had taken place, and felt like crying. But he couldn't even do that.

"Hi, Maria," said the bird.

It had hopped onto its swing and was rocking to and fro.

Having itself a ball.

However hard Sotiris tried that evening, he couldn't recall his classmate having said a word about the bird being able to talk.

Lia had the impression that she'd been in a deep and dreamless sleep. She couldn't recall when it had overtaken her, or what she had done the evening before. Outside it was night. A dull glow filtered through the window into the ward, a rotten half-light that glimmered without illuminating. This was an orange darkness that never turned to real night— she knew too well the darkness of the city. Two beds down from her, the sick woman was snoring as though she'd got a fly up her nose. It was so ghastly waking up in the middle of the night with someone else in the room. *Zzzzz*, went the whistling sound from her nostrils, flat against the pillow. A moment's silence, and then *zzzzz* again. I won't have the time to grow old, Lia thought suddenly. It was a pinch, the thorn of a brief sorrow. No time to get out in the street with a stick and scare the children. To become an old lady with knotty hands and blurry filmed-over eyes.

And what will I be missing? Nothing important. She felt an itch in her arm, and scratched it. The I.V. needle was held in place with a strip of adhesive tape, and this had caused a rash. *Hcnvmb*—what did that mean? *Suspicion of Hcnvmb positive*, that was what had been entered in her file, toward the bottom of the first page, in the Professor's minuscule handwriting. Underlined with a red marker. She'd read through her file as carefully as she could. Till that idiot had come in and stopped her. There'd been nothing new. Test analyses, scans, brief reports from other hospitals, and the diagnosis based on her biopsy. All the same. Her file was overflowing with reports, it took up more room on the shelf than that of any other patient, but had no new information in it. Only that handwritten annotation. Written hastily, on the run. But underlined. Perhaps if she'd been able to stay in the physicians' office a little longer, she might have found out something more. But the Prize Student had caught her red-handed, and started screeching like a hysterical chicken. No, squawking, not screeching. He wasn't capable of screeching. The disgusting fetus. Sexless, too. A sexless fetus. And he'd hit her. Knocked her mouth out of kilter. Her jaw was still numb. But that hadn't bothered her. It was strange. Deep down she might even have liked it. From the moment she saw him walk into the office, with his ridiculous clogs and his stupid frog's eyes, she'd sensed that he was going to hit her. He'd stood over her looking at her as if she were a worm. A worm that had had the nerve to disrupt the order of the physicians' office, to debauch Kalotychos's shrine. But inside he was on fire. On fire and no idea why. A cardboard puppet. With a head like the top of a cock, a swollen red radish. She wouldn't say a word to anyone. A miserable prickhead with the eyes of a beat-up frog. No, she wouldn't tell on him. She'd just let him stew in his own froggish uncertainty.

Suspicion of Hcnvmb positive. Or had it been *positive?*, maybe? Was there a question mark at the end of the note, or not? She wasn't sure. But that had significance, she had to find out. She needed to know. Yet she couldn't remember. She considered getting up and calling Sid, but it was very late and she might worry him. That question mark: she simply couldn't remember. And in any case, did it matter? What could a question mark change? She lay back in bed and tried to recall the appearance of the note in her mind. The tiny letters of the Professor's handwriting jumbled and blurred till they no longer signified anything.

Inside the Banana Moon Sid was aware of having reached that special moment, of having embarked for the further shore, after crossing the boundary from sobriety to drunkenness. With his last gulp of whiskey he'd broken through, and now was floating, iron-gilled, over the heads of the crowd, making dives in among the various groups. These he would split up and reassemble as the fancy took him. The gills were heavy, and tight around his throat, but they helped him stay on the surface. You see that head? It needs to go on a different body. What? I instantly move it to its proper place. And that tall guy with the cap, why has he taken someone else's nose? That nose belongs to the chick with the pointed titties. Give it back to her! Had he said all this out loud? Someone else had spoken.

"Sid!"

"Black Magic…"

"Julia."

"Black Magic!"

"Are you all right?"

"Daba dooba."

"Don't you feel well?"

"Daba dooba. Do you want to daba dooba with me?"

"I'm taking you to the bathroom."

What was going on escaped his attention. There was a click, and they slid into another scene. One that didn't really exist. In the ward where his sister was lying asleep with a black bird on her head. The odd thing was that he knew what was going to happen. What came next in this nonexistent scene. His sister would get up with the bird on her head and tell him to take back the mynah. Have you gone crazy? he would ask her. Because in the room there was no mynah. His sister was lying there dreaming. Let her sleep, don't wake her, that's what he would tell them. Don't torment her, she's very ill.

"Hush now," someone said, "calm down." All he knew was that they'd picked him up bodily and taken him home in a taxi, all of them together— Black Magic, the tall oaf with the white shirt that was now mauve, fishface with his glassy eyes, and P. Then the others had taken off, leaving him and Julia alone together. At one moment he thought he heard her walking up and down the hall, calling "Maria, Maria, where are you? It's Julia—"

That had all happened the day before. Now it was the day after. Sid tossed and turned in bed without coming properly awake. He tried to sit up, but slumped back on his pillow, his head a stone weight on his shoulders. Beside him Julia was still asleep. She'd thrown her clothes off on the floor, and was wearing nothing but a pair of black panties. He'd never seen her before in the morning. Her back was faintly downed, on her thighs and calves were the marks of slapdash shaving, and in some places the hair had begun to grow again. A young body, somehow ungraceful. He gently touched her shoulder and left his hand there. He felt carried off by an avalanche, overwhelmed by an avalanche of tenderness—where had he read that? Was it something his sister had said? Could be. Like when you first try eating snow, and your mouth is crammed full and anaesthetized by the cold and suddenly you bite your tongue without realizing it. Then you're surprised when the snow you spit out is tinged red with blood.

Julia murmured something in her sleep. Sid wriggled over an inch or two on top of the sheets, put his arms around her, and kissed her neck. He felt the fine snow melt in his mouth and burn him. That was that. He felt a numbness in his stomach and his muscles tautened. His body was back. His cock jerked abruptly awake, instantly found its socket. His heart was alert, ready to love, to plunge headlong into that briny snow and catch fire. And then to rise again and fly on a bit further with its burnt wings. He pulled away from her and went to make some coffee.

"The Chinese guy called again yesterday."

This was the first thing she said, the minute she woke up.

"He's a spy from cyberspace."

"Don't start your nonsense again."

She jumped out of bed and began to get dressed.

"Hey, bro, what'll you give me?" Sid asked.

"Tell me."

"No, you tell me first."

"Anything you like."

"I unloaded the mynah on him."

"Say that again?"

"The mynah's at the nurse's house."

"I don't believe you."

"Ask him, then."

"You're the best brother in the whole world!"

· 9 ·

The bus journey was pure hell. At the last moment he'd tried to put his visit off, and had called the village, but Mama Koula wouldn't hear a word of it. He'd been forced to buy a second ticket for the cage, since they refused to accept it for the baggage compartment. He'd put it beside him, and had to hang on to it for the entire trip because it kept sliding across the seat and falling off. And the filthy stuff the bird was munching on, something like sunflower seeds or coarse canary feed, spilled and scattered in the aisle with every lurch of the bus. Everyone kept staring at him as though he were a one-man freak show. It was so hot the sweat was running off his forehead. "Hi there, Maria, hi there, Maria," the bird shrilled, all the way. Nothing would shut it up. Even with his eyes glued on the view outside the window he could feel everyone else watching him. Each time his hand got numb and he changed position to restore its circulation, he'd see the passengers opposite him grin broadly and pretend to be looking somewhere else, and force a silly smile himself. What else could he do? "Hi there Maria, hi there Maria," the bird kept squawking, frantically flapping its wings in its cage. And he kept the silly smile on his face.

"What's this you've got?" said Mama Koula.

The bus had let him off on the state highway, and he'd walked down the road to his house as fast as he could, in no mood to have to give an explanation to anybody. As he approached the built-up area, he stopped near a gas station to catch his breath. The gas station was closed. Just as he was about to pick up the cage and get moving again, he caught sight of the little girl with the longish face. The little girl he'd been stalking that other time down at the old harbor. She was wandering around as though lost. Wearing sneakers with the laces untied. She went over to one of the gas pumps, straddled the thick rubber hose, and tried the handle. All the time she kept biting her lip. Then she jumped down and moved on to the other pump. Sotiris backed off a few paces. He saw a Coca-Cola refrigerator, and hid behind it. He heard her footsteps getting nearer. Now she'll spot the cage, he thought. But the girl marched right past. Sotiris poked his head out and took a covert look. Was it the same girl? How could he be sure? That day at the old harbor was after he'd lost his glasses, and his vision was blurred. Now the girl had gone across to the air pump and was trying it out. "Sssss… sssss," she repeated to herself. She had a strange, rather horsy face. Her legs were thin and tanned. She was wearing a tiny pair of shorts. She gave the equipment a kick and went off whistling. Her shorts were tight in the seat.

"It looks like a rare bird," Mama Koula said.
"A bird of paradise," said his father.

That evening they were expecting a crowd: it was Mr. Papazoglou's name day. "I've had all I can stand," Aunt Lela said when she got back from the beach, "I hope they all eat till they burst today." She threw off her beach robe, sat down on the side of the bathtub, and did her nails in a new shade of pink. In the kitchen it was already evening. A faint ray of light shone unsteadily on the white tiles that Zoe had polished earlier that afternoon. Everything was scrubbed and tidy. Two mounds of coarse-cut potatoes stood on the marble counter ready for frying.

"Don't you dare go and vanish," Zoe told Nina. Nina made as though she hadn't heard. She'd spent the whole day at the seaside, at the shops in the center of the village, down by the old harbor, on the pier; she'd even gone out as far as the fields. She hadn't run into Stephanos. Not anywhere. Her head was going around as though she had sunstroke.

People had started gathering out on the balcony quite early. Friends of Mr. Papazoglou and a few of the regulars. Nina went to the darkest corner, draped herself over the railing, and gazed out at the willows, with their bowed-down branches and silvery leaves. Nothing was the way it had been before. Nothing made sense any longer.

"Nina! Nina!"

I'm not like the rest of you. I'm not a zombie. The word zombie pleased her. At first it sounded funny but then it hit you like a slap. She repeated it several times, rubbing the palm of her hand along the balcony railing. Zombies. Zombies! Stephanos, where are you? How long would she have to put up with their stupidity?

"Nina! Where are you?"

"Just coming—"

She went inside the store and Zoe put a big apron on her that hung right down to the floor. "Don't you dare sneak off again," she said. "Keep an eye on the potatoes, I've got to go outside." She glanced around, scowling, and took off. The oil was spitting desperately in the frying pan and Nina was on her own in the kitchen. "I love you," she told each potato stick before she dropped it in the hot oil. "I love you. And you. I love you all," she whispered, scattering in some salt. A cloud of smoke rose from the frying pan, and the atmosphere in the room grew thick and steamy.

But something was going on outside. A quarrel had started up in the yard behind the store. Sharp, choking voices, followed by a confused noise as though someone had lost his balance and was trying to hang onto a branch to stop himself from falling.

Mr. Papazoglou came into the kitchen from the garden door and walked quickly past her, tucking his shirt into his pants as he went.

About thirty seconds later Aunt Lela appeared, her hair all mussed, looking confused.

"What happened?" Nina asked.

"Shhh," said Aunt Lela. She opened the cupboard, took out a bottle of cognac, and knocked back a glassful at one gulp.

Shhh, she signaled again, one finger to her lips, and wandered out.

"I love you, I love you," Nina told the browning potatoes as she stirred them. She bent over the skillet, and the hot oil spat up at her, burning her face. Thank you, oil, thank you. I'll love you for the rest of my life. I want you to know this.

The bird had become the center of attention. Neighbors had gathered at the house, Mama Koula had brought in a plateful of macaroons, and his father was handing out glasses of ouzo. They'd put the cage on the kitchen table, with a plastic tablecloth underneath, and were standing there admiring it. The bird had settled down beside its water holder, and was watching them out of one eye, not making a sound.

"Sotiris says it talks... pretty-pretty-pretty... go on, say something," Mama Koula told it, pushing her face up against the cage.

One of the neighbors whistled at it, a shrill *fffsstt* made by sticking two fingers in his mouth and capping his tongue.

"Leave sheep to shepherds," said his father. He got a handful of parsley from the refrigerator, thrust it through the bars of the cage, and waved it in front of the bird's beak. Then he began tickling the bird under its wings.

The bird made not the slightest sound, glared with that mean eye at each of them. Its gaze moved around, then fixed on the father. It didn't budge. Its chest was puffed out and its wings moved as though they were breathing.

Sotiris was sitting on a stool with his back against the electric cooker. The way things were developing didn't please him at all. He felt uncomfortable. He wanted to go outside. But where to? He didn't have any place to go. He just wanted to get out of there, take the bird and shut himself up in his apartment, disappear. "Prrrrr..." his father went: he had a whistle in his mouth and the veins in his neck stood out with the effort he was making. It's not a sheep, Sotiris wanted to tell him, it's a bird, you blind or something? Anything beyond sheepfolds and sheepdogs, you don't know shit. But he didn't say a word.

Outside the window the light had begun to fade. Clouds were gathering. Across the strait, Mt. Paliovouna hung in the sky like a giant sack of potatoes, about to burst open and spill into the sea. A couple strolled by on the road outside the front yard. They walked on a little and stopped. The man put his arm round the woman, and they turned away.

Inside the room there was a great shindig going on. People whistled, shouted, called for a little more ouzo. The bird was now curled up on the floor of its cage like a porcupine. Only its eye still glinted.

"Knock that off!" Sotiris said, then realized he'd raised his voice, and lowered it. "Maria makes up her own mind when she wants to talk—"

"Maria!" someone repeated.

"Maria! Maria!" they all shouted in chorus.

Sotiris turned around to see what the couple were doing. They were still gazing at the sea with their arms round each other. Then the man turned the woman's face toward him, holding it in both hands at jaw level. She parted her lips beneath his fingers, and he crammed her entire mouth into his and seemed to be eating her. Sotiris looked away. He stared at Tamvakoula's three-story house—like a chandelier, he thought—and at the sea beyond it, its surface now faintly tinged with white. Half of Paliovouna was now hidden, while the rest was burnt black by the setting sun. His eyes returned to the cage in the room: the sun's last rays were shimmering in through its bars. The bird now had a mocking air, like someone with a private joke, and he remembered Thanási telling him how it played the coquette. Then he remembered that in two or three days he'd be giving it back and would be through with all the bother. When he looked back at the road the couple had gone.

Next morning Aunt Lela suddenly announced that she was going. To take the waters at a spa. The café would be closed for a week. Nina and Zoe were left on their own. Nina spent all day out, walking the streets, down on the waterfront, in the shopping center—for the first time in her life she was free to do exactly what she liked. She encountered Stephanos once only. He was out for a stroll along the harbor, ten paces behind his parents as usual. The moment she saw them, Nina about-faced and marched off whistling. She'd learned to whistle that summer. But inside she felt intensely agitated. Agitated and feverish at the same time.

That night, Zoe pulled down the shutters and stayed in the store. She took the remote control and turned on the television. Nina got a bowl of chilled watermelon from the refrigerator and sat beside her. There was a thriller on, but Zoe picked a program where a bunch of married couples were competing to see which of them were best-matched. At the end of it they got gifts ranging from washing machines to videos. A program for zombies.

"Zoe," Nina asked her, "have you ever kissed with your tongue?"

"I'm sick and tired of you, you know that?" Zoe pointed the remote control and raised the volume.

"Oh go on, tell me. Please?"

"Uh-huh, once."

"What was it like?"

On the screen a husband and wife had put on kangaroo costumes and were hopping around. The studio audience applauded them.

"What was it like?" Nina persisted.

"I don't know, so-so..."

The husband and wife took off their kangaroo

costumes and donned kitchen aprons. Two other couples, hand in hand, were awaiting their turn in a corner of the studio. They stood there pigeon-toed, exchanging frightened smiles.

"Can you show me how they do it?"

"Don't be disgusting."

Nina leaned across and brought her face near that of her sister. From close up Zoe's eye was a giant spitball.

"Come on, let's try it together," Nina pleaded, licking her lips. Her sister's mouth was tightly compressed.

"Leave me alone! I can't stand you any more! I hate you, you know that? I hate you!" Zoe shouted, trembling, and shoved her away.

Nina took the bowl of watermelon and went outside. She sat on the balcony with the lights out. Blackie came over and dozed off at her feet. Every so often he gave a start as some distant sound reached him from the countryside. Nina stroked the cross on her knee. No one had noticed it. The cut had healed, but she could feel the lines of the scar with her fingertips. "You see, Blackie," she explained to the puppy, "he never asked me to love him, I decided to all on my own."

"Psst, psst," came a voice from the garden.

Blackie sprang to his feet. Someone was standing near the willow trees, smoking. The burning tip of his cigarette was moving around like a firefly. Nina stood up straight but couldn't see anything else. "Psst," the voice came again.

Blackie barked, and Nina grabbed him by the

collar to stop him getting loose. The stranger was still standing there. As he inhaled, his cigarette's incandescent tip for a split second created a little light, and she thought she got a glimpse of a sad, doughy face. Then the stranger moved away, his footsteps crunching heavily in the dry grass.

· 10 ·

*W*hen Sid arrived, the ward was empty. It was midday Sunday, and visiting hours had begun an hour earlier. A block of colorless sunlight was coming in through the window and cutting the floor in two. Sid stood in the shaded half and waited. All the beds, except for his sister's, were stripped. Two heads peered in through the doorway, gave a questioning glance, first at the empty beds, then at him, and vanished again. He waited a little longer, and then went to the head nurse's office to ask where Lia was. The head nurse was a middle-aged woman with a sour expression and gray hair done up in a bun. She gave him a mocking look. Or so he thought. "If she's not out on the terrace, you'll find her locked in the bathroom," she said, and returned to her papers.

On the terrace was a young man, leaning over the railing in the full glare of the sun, and smoking. His head was hidden, his body shrunk from the shoulders down. Sid was about to speak to him, but then heard him give a racking cough, and went back inside.

"Lia?" he called.

Not a sound from inside the bathroom.

A man in flip-flops stopped and eyed him reprovingly. Sid waited until he moved off and then asked, again, "Lia, are you in there?"

"Who's that?" Her voice was low and husky.

"Bro."

"Who?"

What had got into her now?

"Isidore. Come on out."

The key turned twice, then once more. The door opened and she fell into his arms.

"How did you manage it?" she asked him. "Tell me, tell me!"

How had he managed it? And how did she always manage to talk as though she was feverish, to always be overexcited? The cause wasn't her illness. She'd been that way since she was a kid. She worked herself up on her own.

"Just a minute," he heard her say, and back she went into the bathroom.

"What were you up to in there?"

"Washing my panties. In biblical peace and quiet."

They went back to the ward. Lia had been unhooked from the I.V. for a couple of hours, and so could move freely.

"Well, come on, talk!" She returned the detergent to the little cupboard under her nightstand, and shut the door.

It was when he'd been sent away to boarding school on the island that he'd begun writing to her. Lots of misspellings, but letters nevertheless. He'd also begun praying. He begged the Virgin Mary to make them come and take him away from there. It was bitter cold, and every morning at six they had to run around the school grounds three times. There was no hot water, that was the English system. Holy Mary, please, I beg you, if you hear me—The bigger boys would wait in the toilets with hangers. *Lia, please, come and rescue me,* he used to write in his letters. In December Lia did arrive, with their parents. There was a north wind blowing, it was a freezing winter day. They'd all had to put on their ties and uniforms for the visitors. He was hoping they'd come to take him away. Lia had made friends with one of the older boys, a sophomore in tenth grade, and she even brought him to the hotel where they were staying, to iron his pants. Sid called her into the bathroom and told her this was one of the gang with the coat hangers. One of the ones who roughed up smaller boys. She went skipping back into the room. The other boy was in his underpants, ironing. "What," she asked him coquettishly, "do you do with the hangers?" Sid was still in the bathroom. He put his hands to his ears and pressed hard till he heard a noise like wasps buzzing. He wanted to lose consciousness, to fall down in a dizzy spell. Two days later his parents and Lia went back home and left him on the island.

"And what's going to be done about the mynah bird?" she asked him when he'd finished his account.

"I'm going to leave it with him."

"For good?"

"For good."

"You're fantastic! You've really cheered me up."

But her cheerful mood soon vanished. Dropped to zero. As usual. A nurse came into the ward to hook up her I.V. again, and Lia stuck out her tongue at her behind her back. After that she became absorbed by the patterns on her nightdress.

"What about your roommate?" Sid asked, glancing across at the empty bed.

"She's been moved to the surgical wing."

"What's her latest thing then?"

"Maternity. She's going to have a baby any minute."

"Spare me the sick jokes."

"I'm serious. She's in surgery right now. They found she's got this thing hanging from her. That she'd grown a tail."

"A small curly one?"

"No, a long bushy one. Like a horse's."

"With ribbons and green spots?"

Lia didn't answer.

"With blonde ringlets?" Sid persisted.

She was staring stubbornly at her nightgown, and gave no sign of having heard him. She didn't want to go on. Her head had gotten smaller, her hair was growing sparsely, unevenly. And her lips had acquired a bluish tinge, something he hadn't noticed on his last visit. I need to have a word with Kalotychos, he thought.

"It's a relief for you, anyway. You're on your own again."

"I don't know…"

Why don't you know? What do you want to find out? Whatever it is, you'll go about it in your own way. For no reason Sid had begun to feel irritated. No reason? No reason.

"So what now?" Lia said.

So what now? she said again to herself. *Hcnmvb*, that's what she was stuck with. *Hcnmvb*. She wondered whether to tell him anything about it. Even though there were other things waiting their turn to be discussed.

"Well, what?" Sid was waiting.

"I was thinking about the mynah, wondering what it'll do now. You think it'll leave its droppings all over the Prize Student's house?" There was something else bugging her.

"You'd better believe it," Sid said.

"Remember Fifi?" she asked him.

"Sure," he mumbled reluctantly. How could he forget her? She was the first girl he'd ever made love with.

"It was five years ago. Five years almost to the day, I think."

He thought hard. "I can't recall the exact date."

"It's today, I think," Lia repeated.

The Octopus Diva, her best friend. Her closest pal at school, all the way through. So beautiful, so vivacious. She was driving like a bat out of hell. Coming back from a party. The car went into a skid, rolled over three times on the highway, rocked to a standstill under the light drizzle, and that was that. At the 186km mark. "The steering column pierced her spleen," she said.

"I don't remember," Sid said.

"She had an internal hemorrhage," Lia said.

"I didn't know about that," Sid muttered.

"If only she'd had her seatbelt fastened..."

"Maybe."

"Or if she'd been fatter, if she hadn't been so terribly thin," Lia went on, working herself up.

It seemed to Sid that the words were cascading straight out of her larynx.

"You know, when it happened I thought, if only she'd had a real belly, a fat flabby belly, the steering column wouldn't have been able to skewer her like that—"

"Please—"

"A fat yellow belly with stretch marks." But Fifi had had the body of a Chinese princess. Flawless. She and Lia had planned together how she'd make love with Sid. They were standing in the kitchen eating chunks of cantaloupe. It was August and their parents were away. There was a heatwave. They were naked, and the fruit-juice trickled down over their breasts. They'd eaten peaches, watermelon, gobbled it all. Fifi kept prowling like a cat between refrigerator, kitchen sink, and table. Sid had shut himself in his room and was feeding his silkworms. This was his special passion that summer. "I'm just crazy about the idea of deflowering him," Fifi had purred. "Well, then," Lia began, and they'd planned the operation down to the last detail. Sid never found out that his sister had been in on it.

"It was bound to happen sooner or later, anyway," he said.

"What do you mean?"

"That she was asking for it, that's what I mean."

"Like how?" Lia was getting angry.

"Fifi was always living right on the razor's edge."

"I never thought I'd hear you say that."

"Whatever."

It was Sunday, so there was no chance of catching Kalotychos in his office. Should he maybe call him at home? But Lia would never give him the number.

There was a short silence. Then Lia said: "Remember when they stopped me from going around with her?"

"When?" he asked in surprise.

"Don't you remember that time when Dad came into my room—you were sitting at my desk writing—and grabbed me by the shoulder and shook me, yelling something about Fifi never setting foot in our house again because if she did he would throw her out by the scruff of the neck, and Mom standing behind him in the doorway looking daggers?"

"No." He had no recollection of this.

"Don't you remember how he turned and looked at Mom as though he was waiting for the password, and then the two of them went out, slamming the door behind them, and I started kicking the walls—?"

What was she leading up to? What was in that mind of hers? "You want me to tell you something you've forgotten?" he cut in. He felt a faint sense of triumph brushing his temples. "You remember how he used to spank us at siesta time?"

"How he—? What do you mean?"

"He had to get really irritated to spank us, had to find some reason to get irritated. Hell, he even used to chase the cats with one of his straw slippers! He'd lie tossing in bed, straining his ear for the slightest sound. Just because he couldn't sleep. He went hunting for noises to get him irritable, so he could jump out of bed in a rage. Sometimes he broke his glasses. We used to communicate like deaf-mutes, in sign language. And walk around on tiptoe. There wasn't a real wall separating the rooms, only a sliding door. We were very careful. If there weren't any noises he would invent one, some minuscule sound he dreamed up in his imagination. Then he'd charge out of his room and whop us."

"I'd forgotten that." Her voice was flat, colorless.

His little triumph faded inside him.

He heard her say: "I have to go to the bathroom." She bent down and took her sponge bag from the nightstand cupboard.

"And I have to be on my way."

But he didn't go. He sat on the bed and waited for her. Outside the window the sun was still high, a pale gray disc in the glowing sky. He stared at the books on the nightstand, the water bottle, the Atkinson's cologne—the same brand that their father used—the cottonwool hanging half out of its packet. Her pillow was folded in two, and had creases. The light was falling on the pillowcase, opening fissures in it.

He tapped on the bathroom door. "Lia—"

"Yes?"

"Will you be long?"

"A while."

"If you're not coming out, I have to go."

"All right."

"See you, then."

"See you, bro."

When Lia returned to the ward, the sick woman was there again, sitting on a chair beside her bed. They must have just brought her back from the surgical wing, Lia thought. Till darkness fell she didn't move from her seat. From the waist up she was swathed in bandages, and her nightdress hung over a swollen shapeless mass. She wore a vague faraway expression.

"They cut them both off," was all she said. After which she uttered not another word all evening. Lia asked if there was anything she wanted, would she like some orangeade? "No," the woman whispered diffidently, her words of thanks almost inaudible. She sat there, head a little bowed, hands outspread, little fingers lightly brushing the hem of her nightgown. It seemed to Lia that she was, almost imperceptibly, rocking back and forth, following some inner rhythm, singing to herself.

She's become like a little girl again, Lia thought before she fell asleep. A little girl from olden times. Quietly waiting in the corner till the others had finished their work before going up and talking to them. Rocking to and fro and singing a silent song to pass the time. Time passes. No one comes. Lia didn't manage to follow this train of thought any further because sleep overtook her and she found herself on a beach.

Fifi motionless, eyes closed, under a scorching sun. Perhaps she's asleep. She's wearing a white-and- blue-striped bikini fastened with knots at her hips. Lia is standing at the edge of the sea with her feet in the water. Further along there are children playing. Their voices, because of the wind, sound clipped and metallic. The beach has become deserted. Fifi's face is expressionless, her mouth shut but relaxed. She's sprawled out on a white towel that's too narrow for her body, and her wet hair is sticking to the stones. A ferry is visible in the distance. As it comes nearer, not perceptibly moving, but more like a series of enlargements of the same photo, Lia reflects that at some point all this immobility will come to an end, and neither of them is prepared for such a thing. They have to hurry, while there's still time. Without opening her eyes Fifi feels around with her left hand for the sunscreen, squeezes some onto her belly, and works it in with her right hand. Lia wants to tell her, "Fifi, you're going to die, don't lie in the sun any longer, let's get out of here." Fifi stretches out her hand again to grab the tube of sunscreen, and remains fixed there in that position. The ferry has arrived, and is there in front of them now, full-size. "Fifi, you're going to die, get up, let's go," Lia says. But in her heart she knows it's far too late.

Sid too is dreaming of Fifi. Dreaming of the same white bikini with the blue stripes. He is lying under the trees in an olive grove. In front of him is an expanse of sea, but all he can see of it are silvery reflections off the water, points of sunlight on the ripples. The light is blinding him. Fifi is sunbathing. He wants to go and talk to her, ask her to meet him somewhere, just the two of them alone, without Lia. He doesn't know how to start this conversation. Or rather, he does know how to start it, but not how to get to the point. Fifi, without opening her eyes, searches around for the sunscreen. Lia comes over, gives it to her, and then stretches out beside her. Sid has grown up but both the girls are still teenagers. They raise their legs high, against the light, toes splayed, cock their heads a little, take aim, and spit, with their toes as the target. That's going too far, it's got to stop—he was the one who taught Lia about spitting contests, that was his trick. And now here she is selling it to Fifi as her own discovery. He has to go and stop her. He stands up and begins to walk down toward the sea. He has to reveal her betrayal, that's his sole concern. As he approaches the beach, the path through the trees becomes steep and narrow. He can hear their laughter in the distance: he can't see them, but he knows they're plotting something. The way down becomes steeper still. He tries to steady himself against an olive tree, its trunk rough with knots and ant holes. He holds onto the branches and edges forward. But something terribly distracting is now happening inside his head. Something has penetrated his ear and is screaming crazily, like a trapped cicada.

"We have special leduced subscliption, celeblating the new millennium," said the Chinese guy.

"What?" said Sid.

"Big leduction—fifty-one weeks, ten weeks glatis, and a cell phone."

"Fifty-one weeks?"

"And a bedsplead."

Sid thought quickly. The Chinese guy's breathing rasped heavily in his ear.

"I have someone in mind who may be interested," he said, and gave him Sotiris's phone number. "Call this number and ask for Maria."

"Malia?"

"Yeah, she makes a specialty of millennia."

"Vely glateful. Thank you."

"Oh, and listen—what's your name?"

"Lee."

"OK, Lee, get this: don't you dare call me up here again, ever."

"Good night."

Sid let his body slump down onto the sofa. He hunted for the remote control, found it, and switched on the television. Clouds were leaving northern Europe and making their way southward. Rain was falling in Scotland. Light confetti was spread all across the Urals. The announcer, a scraggy guy with ripe lips and an incipient bald spot, had a knowing smirk on his face as he spoke, while his outstretched finger indicated cloud formations and troughs of low pressure. A tornado was forming at this very moment over eastern

Europe, sweeping everything along in its path. Asia, Africa and Oceania had sunshine. Sid turned up the volume. "The trough of low pressure is moving southeast," the guy was saying, with a secret glint of triumph. He did pretty well today, Sid thought. Somebody, maybe P., had once told him that the weather forecaster on the news stands in front of a black screen and points here and there on it with his finger without in fact seeing anything. He'd been impressed. What's happening in the Maldives, he wondered, what's going on in the Galapagos? As sleep overtook him, the remote control slipped from his hand.

· 11 ·

The boy is mine… Nina kept trotting from the fridge to the TV to the kitchen and then back the same way. It was Sunday, the middle of the day. She got two or three ice cubes from the fridge and tucked them onto her tummy to melt through her shorts. There was a song on TV, a video clip. The boy is mine… It turned her on. When one of the girls opened the door and smiled at the guy waiting outside, confident that he was hers, the other girl would come onstage and sing the same words in a seductive voice. But the first girl didn't waste any time. With a single lift of an eyebrow she shot him a provocative glance and whispered, with stupendous self-assurance, "The boy is mine"—ho ho, no one's going to steal him from me. Then the second girl would come back, flash her fabulous smile, and repeat the same words in a sweet, intoxicating voice, as though she couldn't care less. Which of them would win in the end? Neither. That was the beauty of it.

"The boy is mine," Nina said. Blackie wasn't interested. He was in one of his fussy moods, searching around for the coolest corner, and every so often giving an irritated yelp.

Zoe had gone upstairs for a siesta. The shutters were half-lowered, and the store was boiling hot in the glare of the sun. The puppy finally crawled onto the tiled kitchen floor, got as far as the front of the refrigerator, and with a tiny whimper flopped there. Nina took a peach and went outside. She'd intended to go to the shopping center, sit on a bench, and eat it. But she changed her mind and made for the old harbor. It was terribly hot, she could scarcely breathe. The air, dry and roasting, seared her nostrils. She took the lane that led past a row of whitewashed cottages and came out on the main street. Not a soul around. The sidewalks were deserted. She went past the pension where Stephanos and his parents were staying. Its shutters were closed tight. "The boy is mine," she whispered, and ran her fingers over the cross on her knee. The heat didn't bother her. Now I'm walking in the desert. I'm a Bedouin. There's a heat wave. On my journey I've seen men dying of thirst. Accepting slavery in exchange for two or three drops of water. I march on with the sun scorching my back. My eyes smart as though I'd rubbed salt into them. I keep moving forward. Everyone around me is dead.

I'm alone in the middle of the desert. Keeping a perfect balance. Marching on.

There wasn't a living soul at the old harbor. The sun beat down vertically. The reeds were crackling in the heat. Nina took the peach from her pocket and bit into it. Now I'm eating the last of the fruit they gave me at the oasis. I've nothing else left. But I'm in no hurry. I'm terribly hungry, my stomach's so starved it's growling, but I just take a small bite and leave it at that. I walk on in the heat keeping a perfect balance. I spit out the peach. I don't need it. Nina spat her mouthful out on the ground. Then she threw the rest of the peach away by the roadside.

There was someone behind the oleanders. They concealed his body, but two tufts of dirty blond hair stuck up above the leaves. Nina walked around the warehouse and scrambled up on some rubble. But all she could see was the guy's back, in a striped shirt, and his wide sloping shoulders. He was hunched forward and holding the branches apart with his hands, as though he was watching something. They've set a horrible trap for me. They're afraid of me, so they've decided kill me. I know their plans. I'm in the heart of the desert and moving forward. Taking care not to make a sound, Nina edged nearer the man from behind. She climbed up on a low wall and tiptoed along it. I know their plans but I'm not turning back. The lions roar hungrily. I'm not afraid. I'm still moving forward, still in perfect balance.

There was a man in jeans and a short-sleeved shirt, with big flapping ears. When he heard her approaching, he turned to face her, and she saw that he was wearing thick-lensed glasses. "Hey," he said, nothing more, and jerked his right shoulder as though it was cramping. "Hey," he said again. Then he looked down at the ground.

His pants were open and his thing was hanging out. It was white with a grayish tinge, like an elephant's trunk. "Don't go," he mumbled. From behind those thick lenses the pupils of his eyes, minuscule and miserable, peered out at her.

"Don't go, I'll pay you," he said.

He took his thing in one hand and began jerking it energetically up and down. "Urrggh," he said after a bit, and stared angrily at the thing he was clutching as though accusing it. "Urrggh," he went again, and continued jerking and looking mad. The sound of an approaching motorbike could be heard from the ring road, with a harsh squeal of brakes at every bend, and as it came panting down the hill, the man seemed for a moment to be moving in time with its rhythm as he puffed and strained, his face distorted by spasms.

Any minute now he'll fall on me, Nina thought. But without their moving the distance between them had increased, the man seemed to have been sucked backwards, into the sun's helix, burning his back, and for a moment or two the space between them shifted among dark shadows and bright objects, among clustering green foliage and fine slender stalks rustling to the distant thrum of the sea.

Suddenly the man stopped moving. His mouth was open, he looked as though he was going to yell or puke. Nina lowered her head. She looked at her shoes, which were old and shapeless, with dirty frayed laces.

"Here," he said, and gave her a worn 1,000-drachma note.

Her face was in light, her body in darkness. She took the money and looked at him. His expression was more relaxed, and there were new shadows round his eyes. A streak of sunlight licked at his sweaty neck. He opened and shut his mouth, his lips moved, but he said nothing.

Nina returned the same way she had come. She scrambled back over the rubble, skirted the warehouse, and jumped over the ramshackle fence, but instead of making for the waterfront, she turned and ran through the reeds. Their thin green shoots completely covered her, and as she moved among them their hairy buds, like little moustaches, brushed her face without scratching it. Above her she could see a hazy clump of clouds rushing with her, and stopping abruptly whenever she did. The sun is out of the blue, she thought for no reason. Life, the world, Stephanos—out of the blue. All of us out of the blue. The sky is out of the blue, I'm out of the blue. I am. I am. I. I.

She was out of breath. The sun was burning her head without being visible anywhere. She ducked under a vault of nettles and found herself in a clearing. Here, in the old days, was where the Labyrinth began. It was a flat patch of land with white stone slabs scattered haphazardly over the dry, packed, reddish earth. The stones looked as though they formed three mazes, and the girls who gathered there in summer to play hopscotch had to jump first onto their left foot, then onto their right, and finally lift both together, never touching the ground. These "mazes" in fact had no exits, and ended by merging at the Sphinx's Mouth, a low stone fountain and the last stop on the hopscotch course. Whoever got there first was the winner. There were other, more complex rules, but she'd forgotten them. Besides, only smart kids were allowed to play—that is, Zoe and her friends.

Now the Labyrinth was just a messed-up clearing. Someone had dug a lime pit in the middle, someone else had traipsed all over the place leaving deep footprints like scars, and the Sphinx's Mouth was dry as a bone, looking as though it had long since ceased to flow. A long procession of ants was carrying a dead maybug, edging slowly forward along the lip of the pit. Nina jumped zigzagging from stone to random stone, but soon got tired. She tried to recall the rules of the game, which were elaborate, incoherent, and mutually incompatible. Rules specially made to trick her since at the time she'd been the youngest. From somewhere nearby came the sound of a rusty pump, and as she emerged from the clearing she saw a man bent over a well, busy pumping, and red-faced from the effort. He filled a bucket with water and lugged it, panting, a dozen or so paces. He stopped in front of a sickly looking fruit tree and emptied out all the water at one go. Then he went back, limping slightly. He gave her an indifferent glance and stooped over the well again.

Nina turned around and made her way back through the Labyrinth. She walked quickly through the fields, which were dried up and overgrown with weeds. She tried to find her way back to the village. Every so often grasshoppers would jump out ahead of her and then vanish again, in a series of big hops. Suddenly she found herself in front of a small patch planted with fresh garlic. It had a wire-netting fence all around it, and its iron gate was padlocked, but a foot or two beyond the gate an opening had been cut, then blocked up with stones. Nina looked at the garlic plants' delicate long narrow leaves, which still contained a little moisture, and seemed as though they were breathing rhythmically in the afternoon light. She moved the stones aside and eased her body slowly under the wire. As soon as she was through to the other side she at once took off her shoes and ran about barefoot to cool the sore soles of her feet.

The low afternoon sun, level now with the garlic shoots, was settling into the sea and finally passing behind the Paliovouna range. The biggest clouds had massed together in the west and were changing color. Orange, red, pink, pale ice-blue and then pink again. The light was radiating an odd glow, without shadows. Nina went back to the fence, slithered through the opening, and left the garlic patch. As she bent down to put her shoes on again, she realized that she was still clutching the guy's 1,000-drachma note. She smoothed it out and sniffed it. It smelt of something. Fish, maybe? No. Some other stuff he'd eaten earlier, dunking bits of bread in it with his hand.

Some kind of food with sauce for sure, she thought, and resumed her walk. She kept going for a long time, till her calf muscles began to ache and she felt hungry.

When she reached the village waterfront, she went straight to the snack stand and bought herself a shish-kebab. Then she sat herself down on the first bench she found. It was early still, and people hadn't yet started coming into the center. Now I'm eating the enemy's shish-kebab. He was on my trail but I shook him off and then I went after him. I got to his hideout and stole all his supplies. He'll starve to death. In his cave I found cured venison and I'm eating it now—but something didn't fit, her shish-kebab wasn't at all like cured venison, which she'd never tried anyway, and suddenly, for some unknown reason, her good mood vanished. She wondered what she did feel at that moment. Nothing. She pinched her arm. What am I feeling right this minute? Nothing. It was amazing. She felt nothing. Only a lightness, the void left by the wind after a storm. She had enough money left for another shish-kebab.

A family of gypsies passed her, laughing and chattering. A little further on they settled down on a stretch of turf, spread open their wax-paper packets at their feet, and began eating grilled meat and tomatoes, while their small children, naked, rolled about on the yellowing grass. Nina got up and moved toward the snack stand. What was missing for her was just one sharp detail. Just one corner-piece missing from the puzzle, that would make sense of that afternoon, make this Sunday different from all the others, and this summer more significant than any before. But what was it? she asked herself as she waited in the line at the shish-kebab counter. She glanced back at Mt. Paliovouna behind her. On the coast opposite the lights of the city dwindled into a glittering swarm of fireflies. What was that one single detail? *I love you, Stephanos* was the first thought that entered her mind. *I love you, Stephanos*: it was so obvious. Yet she felt she'd been transported to some inaccessible place that Stephanos couldn't reach, part of a wholly different story that had nothing to do with him, and at that instant she perceived the astronomical distance now separating them.

· 12 ·

*Y*ou've got to help me," Sotiris said on the phone. Sid exhaled gently, and tried to blow rings with his cigarette smoke, but couldn't. It was hot, and the receiver stuck to his ear.

"You've got to come out to the village with me," Sotiris said.

Sid stared at the little table in front of him. There was a plate on it with a half-eaten slice of bread and a spoonful of marmalade left over from breakfast. Now a fat black fly had alighted on it and was buzzing around the rim of the plate, licking its feelers. "So what's up?" he finally asked.

"A woman—that is, a girl—" Sotiris faltered, and broke off.

"Woman trouble, got you," Sid said, chuckling, and pushed the spoon with his little finger, shifting it well away from the fly, which gave a tiny bob of its head, or rather of its whole body, this being a kind of black solid head.

At the other end of the line Sotiris's breathing sounded nervous and impatient.

"Did you do something to her?" Sid asked.

Sotiris remained silent.

"I don't get you," Sid said.

The fly had pounced on the spoon and was eating away to its heart's content. Sid flicked his cigarette ash on it, but it didn't budge.

"You've got to come out to the village," he heard Sotiris say. "Now, right away—"

Sid turned the spoon over to catch the fly underneath it. It slipped deftly out and went right on eating, quite unperturbed. "What about the mynah?" he asked, after a slight pause, this being the only serious objection to the trip that he could come up with.

"We'll take it with us," Sotiris said.

This summer my life changed, Nina thought. She wrote the phrase down on her pad, and read it aloud. Hmm, just so-so. It struck her as a bit silly. Very silly. This summer was full of sins and *ominous* thoughts, she thought, and promptly wrote this down so as not to forget it. *Ominous* pleased her a lot. It definitely meant something ugly, something dramatic, quiet on the outside but internally terrifying. She liked *ominous* a lot more than *misanthropic*, though she didn't know the meaning of that, either. It was a strange summer, a grotesque summer, a vertiginous summer. Now that was worth the effort, that was a phrase she wanted to remember.

> This summer was filled with sins
> And ominous thoughts
> It was a vertiginous summer
> The boy is mine
> Mine? Yes. Yes! Yes MINE
> With ominous…
> Thoughts
> Words
> Phrases
> Words hunting thoughts
> Pauses
> In the eyes' lost pupils

"Nina! Nina!"
"Coming!"
  She hid the pad and hurried back to the yard, where Zoe was calling her.

"How did you get me tangled up in this?" Sid asked. He was calling from a phone booth on the waterfront, in the village. In front of him shimmered a glassy sea that stretched out as far as the opposite coast, under the lee of the broken-off mountain.
  "I can't hear you very well," said Lia.
  "I'm out at his village, that nurse of yours dragged me out here—"
  Lia said: "That woman in the next bed to mine—she died."

Sid remained silent.

"You know what she said to me the afternoon before?"

"What?" Sid swallowed nervously. He eyed a barrow just down the road selling cotton candy.

"She'd just come back from the bathroom, she walked into the ward waving a roll of toilet paper like a club, and you know what she said to me, triumphantly? 'A shit a day keeps the doctor away.' She was glowing all over."

"And so?"

"And so, she was fine, and an hour later she was dead."

"Yes. I see."

"She'd changed a lot after the mastectomy. She'd become sort of—"

"Sort of what?"

"Like a little girl."

"Don't let it upset you."

"Why do you say that?"

"I hate it when you're upset."

"You don't understand a thing. I'm not upset. I couldn't care less whether that—that bloated tick died or not..."

She'd wanted to tell him how the whole thing happened, but she no longer felt like it. The sick woman had come back from the bathroom brandishing a roll of toilet paper. She'd said to her, with vast satisfaction, "A shit a day keeps the doctor away," and got into bed. Lia was reading. How much time passed? It must have been getting near dinnertime, because she thought she could make out the noise of the carts slowly grinding into action at the far end of the corridor. She heard something like nonstop hiccupping from the next bed. "Are you all right?" she asked, without looking up. There was no reply. The hiccuping went on.

When she turned to see what was going on, the patient had doubled over as though seized by cramp. She brought one hand to her mouth, but too late to stop a yellowish, bloody clot of spittle from sliding down her chin. Then a violent spasm shook her body, and her mouth gaped wide open. She let out a muted belch, then threw up blood and mucus. She tried to raise herself up from her pillow, but fell back again, choking, unable to breathe.

Lia jumped out of bed, went to her, took one of her arms and raised it above her head. She tried to lift the other arm, but a torrent of viscous gray slime gushed from the woman's mouth and spread down her white nightgown.

The crisis seemed to be over: it had lasted no more than a minute. Lia wiped the woman's mouth and nose and hurried out of the ward. She ran down the corridor. At the far end the door to the service stairway was open and a trolley laden with dishes just squeezed past her. Through the window of the head nurse's office she caught a glimpse of a nurse with a cup of coffee in her hand and a newspaper spread out in front of her. "Please—come quickly—"

The nurse got up at once. Lia stayed where she was, standing in front of the doorway, staring through the glass partition at the inside of the office.

Behind her she heard voices and the sound of hurried footsteps. A loaded trolley went by, its wheels screeching as it rounded the corner. From some other floor came the sound of water being run hard into a sink trap. Then a water pipe whistled. A door opened with an almost inaudible creak, and then began to swing slowly shut again, the creak getting louder all the time, till it merged into the rumble of a broken toilet cistern.

How long did she stand there? She had no idea. When she returned to the ward there was no one there. A screen with plastic curtains hid the sick woman's bed. Lia went over and drew back the curtain. The woman's back was propped up by pillows. Her arms lay slackly on the sheet, but with the fingers a little tense and outstretched, as though about to lay hold of their own body. Her head had changed, too, had shrunk, and a thin wisp of stray hair stuck up from it like an Indian topknot. Her eyes were closed, the eyelids heavy and crinkled. Her mouth was half open, her voice cut short in mid-cry. Her chin was no longer visible, and her lower lip had been sucked in. On the nightstand stood a glass of water, and in it was a gleaming lower denture, with five large teeth set into vibrant pink plastic flesh. "My teeth are the only healthy part of me left," the sick woman used to boast, running her tongue in demonstration over her bright white incisors. The plate, that was her secret. A secret that was now, along with various food particles, floating almost motionless in the water.

"Come out this minute! What are you doing in there?"

It was Dr. Kalotychos, in a freshly ironed white gown and black English shoes.

"O.K..." Lia closed the curtain.

Out, out, he gestured, his eyes on the door. "All right," she said reluctantly, and left.

Sid was taking a solitary stroll along the waterfront. Sotiris had gone off to help his father in the orchard. Sid still hadn't managed to find out the reason for his trip to the village, but that didn't bother him overmuch. He felt lighthearted, and never mind any worries lurking behind the door: his feet were taking him wherever they liked. It was good to be walking beside the sea again: he'd missed the brisk, hot breeze blowing landward intermittently in the wake of the waves, the little gusts of wind that ruffle your hair, warming your head and burning your face. Three old men were sitting on a bench, silently watching the bustle of activity around the boats, the picture of perfect happiness. What was that you said? Just that: that was the way he'd like to grow old. To sit in the sun and breathe the good air and let the world go by. To watch things: first a fisherman hauling his nets off his boat, cursing under his breath, then a lame seagull's progress, then a small child with a half-eaten roasted corncob. Then nothing. Without passion or excitement. To be conscious of nothing beyond the knots in the bench where he was sitting, his hands on the wood; to trace the grain of the wood with his fingers, to have that as his sole excitement.

And at night? The tick-tock of the clock will fill his room, but will no longer have any meaning. Time will expand, become a single boundless moment. On the ceiling he'll see a mosaic of light and shadow, boats crossing it from one wall to the other, the glimmer of a seagull by the window; the lights of cars from the road will riddle the slatted blinds for brief breath-catching moments. He will be watching the same scene as this morning, except that then he'll lie back in bed and following the action by letting his gaze wander whenever it pleased. His hands will slide gently over the cool sheets. Without emotion, with no feeling. His fingers will play with the coarse material, feel its bare impersonal texture. Their movement will be mechanical, absent-minded. He will caress the sheet, look up at the ceiling. For hours on end. He'll pull up one corner of the sheet, wrap it around his head, and smell it. He'll lose himself in an indefinable state, something at once sweetish and tinged with sourness. He'll feel a slight touch of faintness. Because Julia will be there. Julia is still here. The well-worn sheets are straightened out now but have kept the outline of her fresh body. He wants to embrace her, but he feels embarrassed because he knows he's already got a hard-on, and he draws back. The briny snow melts in his throat and burns it.

Without realizing it, Sid had walked all the way to the village square, and come to a halt in front of the taxi stand. The place was a hive of activity. Women with cropped black hair were hurrying to and fro, taking shortcuts between the tables of the single patisserie, small plastic handbags tucked tightly under their arms. The waiters bustled around them, sweating, shouting orders to one another, while the black-suited owner, balancing an empty tray in lieu of a hat, barked instructions to the surrounding air. A cluster of people had gathered under the shade of the awning and were impeding movement: they just stood there rooted to the spot, staring in front of them and looking lethargic.

"Make way! Step aside there!" A taxi driver, laden with baggage, was flailing a path for himself through the crowd, followed by a thin, sallow-faced man with a little pot belly. Behind him came a plump woman with a sideways glance. The taxi driver dumped his load by the hood of the car and let out a sigh of relief. The man turned and said something to the woman, who looked back over her shoulder and nodded. A young boy was standing a little further along, beside the kiosk, gazing out to sea. Sid was very near him, and noted his obstinate expression, the beautiful dark eyes that stared straight ahead without noticing anything.

"Stephanos!" the woman whined.

The boy didn't move, but his chin twitched, almost imperceptibly. He hates them, Sid thought. "Stephanos!" the man repeated, an edge of impatience in his voice, "we're leaving—" The boy didn't budge. Sid watched the barely detectable changes of expression on his face. He hates them with every bone in his body, he thought, and at that precise moment someone else caught his attention. This was a young girl in red shorts across the street, near the shop-front of the patisserie. She was standing on one leg, like a pelican, and observing the same scene, not missing a thing.

"Stephanos!" The thin man's patience was exhausted. The woman had got into the taxi and was waiting, one hand holding the door open. The boy reluctantly came over. Sid looked across in the direction of the girl, and saw her turn on her heel and take off, her hands in her pockets. It reminded him a little of the way Lia used to walk when she was just a kid—two steps, a quick skip, two more steps. A hop, a nonchalant pace forward, another hop. He heard the trunk of the taxi slam shut, followed by both doors, one after the other. The driver took his seat, and the car set off, with a drawn-out melodious toot of its horn. Through the open window Sid could see the boy. He was sitting in the middle, his indifferent gaze fixed on the back of the driver's neck. A few yards further along, among the loafers around the patisserie, the girl reappeared. As though magnetized, her eyes never left the receding taxi till it vanished. Then she shoved her hands back in her pockets and walked away whistling.

Sotiris suddenly appeared and caught Sid by the sleeve. "That's her!" he exclaimed. He shoved Sid behind the kiosk. "That's her!" he repeated.

"You've got to be kidding—"

"Stay behind here, don't let her see you," Sotiris whispered, without letting go of Sid's sleeve.

But the girl had already reached the far side of the square, her tight shorts now just a red blob moving quickly in the direction that the taxi had vanished.

"She's just a kid," Sid said softly. He glanced around the square, at the people bustling to and fro with their shopping, at the cabs lining up at the taxi stand. Then he turned and faced Sotiris, who looked away. "Twelve, thirteen at the most," Sid added, with a sad smile.

But Sotiris paid no attention to him: he was shaking all over. The veins in his throat had swollen, and when he began to speak it was in a confused jabber. His speech was garbled, he chomped his words, he lurched from one subject to another. Sid listened without comment. Wait long enough, and some kind of sense would emerge from this confusion. Sotiris reminded him how, during their first meeting, at the patisserie near his home, he'd promised he could count on him for whatever he needed—"money, a woman, even to beat someone up," repeating his actual words verbatim, a statement Sid himself had forgotten.

"Well, what do you want of me? I don't understand," Sid cut him off, annoyed.

"I want you to—get rid of her," Sotiris said, not meeting his eye. His chest was heaving irregularly, and greasy with sweat. Now that he had managed to express what it was he wanted of Sid, he seemed inflexible.

"What's that supposed to mean? Are you nuts?"

"The one thing I know is that I know nothing," Sotiris said, and fixed his gaze on some plastic toys hanging outside the kiosk.

"No argument there," Sid said. He remained silent for a moment, then made one last attempt to bring the situation into some kind of logical context. "All right, I'm supposed to get rid of her. But for what reason? Tell me—"

"The one thing I know is that I know nothing," Sotiris repeated. End of discussion.

If someone could see us at this moment, Sid wondered, what on earth would he think? Sotiris was carrying a pickaxe and a coil of rope, Sid a hammer. The only thing he'd managed to get out of was bringing along the hatchet from the henhouse and the kitchen chopping knife: these might attract attention, an argument with which he'd got Sotiris to change his mind. Sid thought about P., who, if he'd seen him equipped like this, would have raised one eyebrow and smiled in that ironic way he had, and then about his sister Lia, who'd got him mixed up in this business to begin with. They'd waited in Sotiris's house, along with his parents, until darkness fell. His father was a boring know-it-all, his mom nice enough. They'd watched television and eaten a dish of kid in lemon sauce while they waited. And now they'd gone out, with their equipment, into the starry night.

The girl lived near the sea, in a rather isolated neighborhood. There was a distillery, a vacant lot, and her house: the village came to an end there. And it wasn't a private house, but a coffee shop, a store raised off the ground, rather long and narrow, with roll-down shutters along the front and a low veranda hidden by willows. The upper floor had clearly been added later, and still looked half-finished.

They approached slowly, without speaking, and came to a halt under the trees. The house was blacked out, and gleamed in the moonlight like a capsized boat. Everything was still and silent. Sid could distinguish Sotiris's heavy breathing from his own, which was lighter and slightly uneven. From somewhere in the background came the persistent sound of the waves surging in over seaweed. "Sshh," Sotiris said, as though straining to hear something. Then he turned and began walking toward the sea. A sparse clump of reeds hid the shoreline. "Sshh," he said again. He put down the rope and the pickaxe, and parted the reeds with a gentle movement, as though afraid they might break.

The girl was wading out into the sea with her clothes on. The water had come up as high as her knees. Sid could make out a small black dog standing at the near edge of the seaweed, the line of its outstretched muzzle clear against the darkness. Lia is going to have to pay for this, he thought. But how to make her pay? Ah, fuck it. When he'd realized she was the brains behind the whole business with Fifi he'd beaten her up. Kicked her from behind, between her legs, right in the crotch, that had doubled her up, leaving her speechless with pain. He knew she was the brains, but couldn't figure out precisely what her role was. That was what made him so mad, the fact that he suspected, was virtually certain of, her involvement, yet didn't understand exactly what was going on. One other time he'd found her at her desk, writing, and he'd smacked her head right down onto the wood. She wasn't expecting it, when she saw him come in she gave him her usual teasing smile. Life isn't just one long joke, that's what he'd wanted to get across to her.

But he was a kid, he didn't know how to say it, so he beat her up. He'd opened up a gash in her head, split her eye socket. They'd rushed her off to the hospital, she got two stitches. She still had the scar.

Sotiris nudged him gently. The girl had come out of the water and was walking barefoot in the direction of the house. They picked up their tools and followed her. She skipped up onto the veranda and turned to see if the dog was following her. "Blackie!" she called in a tremulous voice. She sat down on a canvas-backed deck chair, and the dog came bounding after her and curled up at her side. The girl tucked her feet up under her on the deck chair and rested her chin on her knees. Then, suddenly, she burst into tears. "Now," Sotiris whispered in his ear, and advanced toward the veranda. The coil had come undone and one end of the rope was dragging along the ground. If I was an American hero, what would I do now? Sid wondered, feeling the weight of the hammer in his hand. American hero my ass. A super-cretin, that's what he was, a failed stuntman in a scene that was completely ridiculous.

By now they were very close, their bodies within touching distance of the veranda railing. The girl was right in front of them, only a hair's breadth away. Her bare legs were drawn up on the deck-chair. She had her arms clasped tightly round her knees, and was rubbing them with thin, nervous fingers. Her sobs had become louder: she was crying, now, in a heartrending manner, and one side of her face, all streaked with tears, glistened in the moonlight. Suddenly the dog sprang to its feet and growled in their direction. "Now," he heard Sotiris repeat, in a dull, flat voice. With his free hand Sid caught him by the arm and motioned him to wait. Under the hot, sweaty skin he seemed to sense Sotiris's blood raging impatiently through his veins. The dog came at them, growling again. "I'll deal with the dog, you get the girl," Sotiris muttered, trying to shake his arm free. Above their heads a window opened. "Is that you, Nina?" a voice asked.

Sid was still clutching Sotiris's arm. Do something, quickly, he told himself. The hammer slipped from his hand and dropped to the ground, striking the concrete gutter. The noise was slight, but quite audible.

"Who's there? Nina!" the voice at the window called out again.

The girl dropped her feet to the floor and stood up. Sid just had time to see her come to the railing, shivering a little, her vision clouded with tears. Then he became aware of Sotiris's face, now turned completely in his direction, staring at him, frozen in baffled doubt, till Sid pulled him violently by the arm and they began to run. "Help! Help!" screamed the voice from upstairs. The dog pursued them for a little through the willows. For a moment Sid got the impression it was hanging onto the cuff of his pants, but he wasn't sure. It fell back behind them, panting, and just gave a couple of weak barks.

I'm done for, Sotiris thought. They were getting near his neighborhood: the low whitewashed houses were all deep asleep. From inside the little square yards the smell of basil hit his nostrils and made him nauseous. Beside him Thanási was panting in exhaustion. He'd begun to drag his feet, he couldn't go on running.

"Why was she crying?" he suddenly asked.

"I don't have a clue," Sotiris said.

"What did you do to her?" Thanási asked again, and came to a sudden halt. He leaned against a telephone pole to catch his breath.

"It's not what you think," Sotiris answered vaguely. He ought to have been angry with his friend, but he felt no anger, just overwhelming disappointment. Thanási was far less courageous than he'd made himself out to be. Just a wretched coward like himself, scared shitless, and worse. Except that he, Sotiris, knew the score about his own nature, and didn't talk big and fantasize like his old classmate. He couldn't rely on him: he'd learned that, all right. But the lesson had come very late. And now what was he to do? Because the girl was going to tell on him, that was certain. The whole village would pick up his scent. He'd be a laughing stock. And he was going to have to explain things to his parents, but what could he tell them? He was really done for. "Come on, let's get a move on," he said, through gritted teeth.

They finally reached his house. He slid the front gate open silently. His knees felt weak and his head was burning. He heard the sound of the television in the dark: his parents watched it with the light off to keep mosquitoes away. Whatever happened, they couldn't see him in this state. He had to win himself a little time, do some thinking before next morning.

"Don't talk," he whispered, "come on over here," and pushed Thanási in the direction of the henhouse.

Inside it, the heat was intolerable. They sat on the straw, jammed up close side by side. For a little while they remained silent, trying to get used to the revolting stench. "So what do we do now?" Thanási asked. "You tell me," Sotiris said spitefully. You who promised me the moon and the stars, he thought, but didn't say. He waited for his classmate to react to his resentful tone, but nothing happened.

They fell silent once more. Every so often the hens would stir without waking. Maybe they were having bad dreams, maybe some rooster had designs on them, but whatever their troubles were, they weren't really bothered... The smell in there was disgusting—chickenshit, urine, rotting straw, yet they still slept the sleep of the just. Nothing bothers these hens, Sotiris thought, they don't have a worry in the world. It can rain or snow outside for all they care. I'd be better off as a hen than stuck in this mess. This ghastly mess. He felt an impulse to get up, grab one of them, and wring its neck, strangling it there in the darkness before it could let out a peep. He lifted the pickaxe from where it lay at his feet and balanced it in his hand. "What are you up to?" Thanási asked. His voice sounded uneasy. Sotiris said nothing, kept the pickaxe in his hand. This was what he was going to dig the girl's grave with. It wouldn't have taken much effort, she was so small and skinny. By now the whole business would have been over if they'd carried out his plan. She'd be buried, and he'd have a load off his mind. No one would have been any the wiser. Just one more missing kid, big deal, tons of them disappearing daily, using TV to look for them but never finding any. And now she'd be reporting him. She was going to ruin his life. Dr. Kalotychos would find out about it too. At the thought of the Professor he became panic-stricken, and almost automatically his thoughts turned to the halfwit from Ward 11, he remembered the scene in the office, the way he'd clouted her. It was that little weasel who was to blame for everything. From that day on everything had gone wrong for him. He'd become a different person. Something had snapped inside him and now he was running at a hundred miles an hour, unable to stop. He didn't recognize himself. He felt a pang of anxiety, as if someone had him by the throat and was squeezing but not quite strangling him. One after another, events whirled around in his mind, pulsed crazily against his temples. He really was done for. Again he recalled the girl's horsey face among the oleanders, her tight red shorts, the way she stared at him that day down at the old harbor. The direct piercing glance she gave him when she took the 1,000-drachma note. Hey, wait a minute. She'd taken it. That was a significant piece of evidence. Why hadn't he thought of it earlier? Possibly she wouldn't report him after all. Possibly. Just possibly.

"Have you seen *Zelig*?" he heard Thanási ask him.

Sotiris, still lost in his own thoughts, gave him a questioning look in the darkness. The stink of the henhouse was now reaching him from inside himself, along with his own breath.

"It's about this Jew who's a contemporary of Hitler," Thanási went on. "He's very wealthy and spends all his time traveling—"

What's he unloading on me now? Sotiris wondered. Could he be losing it?

"He's highly impressionable, he's influenced by everyone he meets," Thanási continued, "he travels all round the world distributing handshakes right and left, meeting all the big celebrities—"

"Is this a joke?"

"No, a movie. So he goes to see the king of England, and after the audience is over he comes out talking with an Oxford accent, you know how the Brits speak, puckering up their mouths like a hen's ass. And when he emerges from Hitler's Chancellery, he grows a little moustache and begins barking like Hitler—"

"Woof, woof," Sotiris went, and held his breath for a moment.

"Right," said Thanási. "And when he visits China, his eyes go slanty and he talks like a Chinaman, and then he goes—"

"Me too, I have this Chinese guy who calls me every evening," Sotiris said, interrupting him.

Thanási took no notice. "And when he goes to see the French president, he comes out talking with a French accent," he said, and burst into a fit of nervous laughter. "I zink you awe vewy attwactive—get it?"

"Get what?" Sotiris asked. He was beginning to get nervous and irritated.

"Zelig—the word means 'chameleon,' " Thanási explained listlessly. His enthusiasm had evaporated.

"And what's that got to do with us?"

"I don't know, it just came into my head," Thanási told him. After that he didn't speak again.

He's got a problem, Sotiris thought. That explains everything. He's not in his right mind. I had a hunch about it the very first time I met him. He could always ask one of the doctors at the hospital about this case. If the girl didn't report him. If he didn't lose his job. He got up and felt around blindly for the door. He pushed it open and stuck his head out. There wasn't a sound to be heard. His parents had gone to bed. They could let themselves into the house.

"Your classmate? He's at least five years older than you," said Mama Koula the next morning, while shaking sheets out of the window. Sotiris grunted something unintelligible. He didn't feel like talking. He had slept like a log for ten hours and still felt he'd woken up too soon.

"Hi there, Maria," chirped the mynah from the refrigerator. It was out of its cage and circling around as it pleased, taking off over their heads.

"You just sit quiet," Mama Koula told it. She was still thinking. "What am I saying?" she said to herself after a while. "Five years? More like ten."

"Leave sheep to shepherds," said his father as he came in. The classmate was Sotiris's business and she shouldn't stick her nose into it.

"Render unto Caesar the things that are Caesar's, right?" This was Thanási speaking. He came into the kitchen just at that moment, giving the father a meaningful glance.

"Right you are!" said the father, with a cheerful laugh, and gave Mama Koula a look that meant it was high time to fix some coffee.

It's a good thing that my father gets on with him, Sotiris thought. At the very least, his classmate was a decent guy. A bit prone to exaggerate, a bit over-sensitive. And given to fantasizing. But above all a good friend. Together they'd face whatever was going to happen. The events of the night before came crowding back into his mind like a sharp blade through his heart. But now he had a friend at his side. That meant something.

· 13 ·

*P*hysical decay starts in an odd fashion. With no warning. The way Scandinavians get drunk. One minute they're talking to you quite normally, the next they're throwing up on you. The way your body quits is much the same. One day you're fine—well, more or less fine. The next, one after another your organs begin to go on the blink. At first it's just a twinge or two in your neck. A voice whispering to you when no one's there. Then your left hand goes numb for an hour. For two hours. For a whole day. Your sense of touch comes back at some point, but it's not the same. For no reason you get shivering fits, every now and then, or bouts of pins and needles. A familiar noise reaches you, muffled in cottonwool and transformed into something terrifying. The ticking of a clock grows thick in the air, dominating the entire room. "Stop talking," Lia said. "I didn't say anything," someone replied. Lia opened her eyes. Dr. Kalotychos was standing in front of her. "It must have been voices from outer space," she said, and smiled.

"There was something I wanted to talk to you about," Kalotychos began.

Lia sat up in bed. It struck her that the doctor was looking at her in an uneasy way. Perhaps the appropriate moment had come.

"There's something come up—I wanted to run it by you first—" he started off again, with an effort, and then fell silent.

"Would that something happen to be *Hcnvmb*, by any chance?" she asked suddenly, looking him straight in the eye.

"How did you find out about that?"

"I found out."

"I have to know."

"No, I have to know."

"It was suspected, but we haven't had any confirmation yet," he said, hedging. He had a disappointed expression, as though *Hcnvmb* was the best possible thing that could happen to her.

"I don't believe you."

He looked at her and said nothing for a moment. "Actually, what I wanted to discuss with you is this. There's another patient, an elderly lady... I don't have a bed for her in another ward. I know you asked to be on your own, after the last one—" He cleared his throat in embarrassment. "The thing is, I have no alternative, that's why I wanted to ask you. You see how we've been spoiling you here," he concluded, with an artificial smile.

"No problem," Lia said.

"Who told you about the virus?" he asked again.

"It doesn't matter, forget it," Lia said, and sank back onto her pillows. From the corner of her eye she saw him studying her thoughtfully. "You can bring the new patient in whenever you like," she added, and closed her eyes.

"Hey, bro—" Sid whispered.

"Yes?" said Lia.

But he didn't hear her.

"Bro—" he said again, very gently, bent over her.

Lia heaved herself up on her pillows. She had a fever and felt constantly fatigued. Now even getting words out properly required enormous effort. She smiled up into Sid's face, hanging there above her: she was always surprised by that expression of his, like a cat's, a cat that's been brought up among dogs. His mouth always shaped like a question mark above his chubby chin.

"How are you?" he asked her.

"If it weren't for this bitch of a fever we could have ourselves a great time," she said in a low voice, then indicated the new patient's bed with a glance. "Now there's a character." The woman had been moved into the ward the day before, together with her own private nurse. She imagined she was on holiday in a hotel, and that the nurse was her chambermaid. The doctors were waiters, and Kalotychos the manager.

Sid took a look at the old lady, who was gazing expressionlessly into space, and at the nurse, who was sitting silently on a stool by her bedside, working at a crossword. Neither of them had noticed his presence. He turned back to Lia. "How high is your temperature?" he asked.

"Don't know," she whispered.

They fell silent. The nurse got up, administered two spoonfuls of water to her patient, and settled back on the stool.

"What's happening with the mynah?" Lia asked after a little.

"Oh bro, the mess you got me into over that—" Sid started off. He was all set to tell her every detail of what had gone on in the village, but before he'd even finished his description of the nurse's home, including the henhouse, his parents, and the mynah prinking around the place as cool as you please, like a samba queen, he noticed that Lia's eyes were closed, and he wondered whether she was following what he said. Her breathing was regular, but a little fast. Her chest rose and fell normally. Could it be that she was no longer interested in the nurse's affairs? At the back of his mind panic lurked; it seemed foolish to try and ignore it. Panic and fear, he knew very well, had been there right from the beginning of his visit. He stood up noiselessly, cocking an eye at the bed with the old lady in it. His eye met the nurse's, and he nodded at her, but she made no response to his greeting, and he left the ward.

Dr. Kalotychos was sitting in his office examining a file, a preoccupied expression on his face. When he saw Sid come in he told him to sit down, and returned to his papers.

It was a long, narrow, well-lit room, with two big windows and built-in bookshelves laden with files. A rectangular screen of opaque celluloid covered the one free wall. There was a white gown hanging from a hook on the door. The doctor's desk was a large, plain formica table, flanked by two gray metal chairs for visitors. Directly opposite the desk, on the other side of the room, a light blue standard fan was on full blast, turning to and fro on its base in a 180-degree arc, and radiating powerful currents of tepid air all around the room. For a while Sid observed the palm of the doctor's hand change position at regular intervals, holding down the stack of papers for the fraction of a second that the breeze lasted, and then returning to the desk when the air current moved on.

At last a nice little guy: that was how Lia described him. About sixty, nervous and somehow impatient. Firm, pink skin, restless eyes behind gold-rimmed glasses, and babyish ears. Well-cared-for fingers beating a tattoo on the desktop, which, except for a telephone and a glass paperweight, was empty. Not even a speck of dust on it. Inside the paperweight was a fossilized tadpole, on the verge of becoming a frog, in a pose suggestive of prayer. Interesting case, Sid thought. Now I can see why my sister likes him.

"Have you notified your parents?" the doctor asked him suddenly, leaning slightly forward.

Sid shrugged vaguely. "There aren't any parents," he said. The stream of air touched his back fleetingly and moved on.

Kalotychos seemed unsatisfied by this answer. The telephone on his desk rang, a shrill and startling note, but he kept his eyes on Sid expectantly.

"They're very old," Sid muttered. "They live out in the provinces." The warm air current came round behind him again, and he felt a kind of shock between his shoulder blades, a faint tremor that pierced him momentarily and faded inside him.

"I see," Kalotychos said. He reached out a hand and picked up the receiver. When he spoke it was with considerable irritation. He gave brisk instructions to one of his assistants, and then turned back to Sid.

"The thing is, it's a new virus," he said, as though resuming a conversation they'd left unfinished. He pulled out a clean sheet of paper from the stack in front of him and scribbled something that looked like a small cockroach.

"Could it possibly be a case of—?" Sid began, but got no further. The doctor's scribble told him nothing. It might even really be a cockroach or some other bug. Suddenly he felt trapped there in his chair. He waited for the gust of air from the fan to come round behind him again, and prod him into asking those questions that had been tormenting him for the last few months. The hum of the fan was now clearly audible, yet the air stream was taking its time.

"If what you have in mind is HIV, the virus that causes AIDS," Kalotychos explained, "it's not that at

all. To put it crudely, it's the exact opposite of HIV."
His eyes glinted momentarily behind his glasses. "For
reasons still unknown to us, the immune system
becomes so intensely active that it destroys the
body's organs. Look at this—" He drew a kind of ring
framing the cockroach. "The organism arms itself to
fight a virus that doesn't exist. A wholly imaginary
virus. Why the body should suddenly decide to
attack a nonexistent virus is a question to which at
present we have no answer. To put it in simple terms,
it becomes a Don Quixote: it calls up all its defense
forces, and then turns them against itself."

As he listened to the doctor, Sid found he couldn't
fix his mind on anything. He was having trouble
concentrating, the more he tried, the more he felt his
attention wandering, being sucked up into some
unknown location or perhaps into nowhere at all.

"What interests us—that is, concerns us—about
your sister's case is, precisely, the absence of a virus.
Do you follow me?" Kalotychos concluded, looking
at Sid with sympathy.

"Yes, I understand," Sid said. But he didn't
understand a thing. At that moment he'd much rather
have been alone. Putting his fingers in his ears and
shutting out every sound. Everything was without
rhyme or reason, off the map, out of sync. The
whirring of the fan, nonstop and very audible, the
way in which its circular motion suddenly intensified
the sound in this brightly lit room—all this swept him
away into a whirling-dervish mental spin, sent him
back, back, into the distant past. Back to some long-
ago summer. He was with his sister in her room, and

they were playing the game "My Slave, Your Slave." One day he would do everything Lia wanted, trotting round to the kiosk for ice cream, tidying her desk, spying on her girl friends. Next day it would be her turn. But she never kept her part of the bargain. Most times she fooled him: she'd act as his slave for no more than an a hour or so, after which she'd find some excuse, provoke a fight, and vanish.

"So that is the famous *Hcnvmb* virus," the doctor said with a nod. He stared thoughtfully for a moment at the paper with his sketch on it. "And you'll see," he added, suddenly frowning, "it won't be long before everyone's talking about it, it'll be the topic of the day. And they'll nickname it Anti-AIDS, I have no doubt whatsoever about that." His lower lip trembled slightly with suppressed indignation. "Nonsense! People are really quite incredibly ignorant, especially the ones who work for the mass media. When it comes to misinformation, these gentlemen are the real criminals! Because, you see, *Hcnvmb* is much worse than that—it's crafty, insidious—"

Two nurses were standing outside the ward having an animated discussion. One was the new patient's private attendant. Her back was narrow and slightly rounded. As Sid passed behind her he noticed a swelling under her collar, as though fat had accumulated around the nape of her neck. Somewhere he had read that this was called a bison's hump.

Inside the ward Lia had perked up again. She was sitting up in bed and seemed to have recovered her strength. She signaled sharply to him with her hand to come on in. Seeing her waiting so impatiently, Sid wondered what to tell her about his meeting with the doctor.

"I saw her naked," she said, as soon as he got there.

"Who?"

"The nurse. Are you asleep on your feet?"

"Tell me everything," he said, with an effort to smile at her.

"This morning she went into the bathroom to freshen up. I didn't know, and I opened the door— she hadn't locked it. I just stood there with my mouth open. She was half naked. A really statuesque body, knockout breasts, dark nipples like nut chocolate, you'd have flipped. But there was one really awesome thing—"

"Tell!" said Sid eagerly, standing at the foot of the bed.

"The really awesome thing... Well, she was wearing black silk garters. On her panties there was the picture of a cobra that ended in a woman's bright red mouth dripping blood between her thighs... and a bunch of nasty sharp teeth were sticking out of the mouth—"

"And a green forked tongue?"

"You don't have a clue, do you? I'm being serious, I tell you that woman's a real volcano. Anyway—" she said, and fell silent.

Two beds further down the old lady was asleep, hands folded on her breast. The nurse's head poked in briefly through the doorway. She gave a sulky glance at her patient and withdrew again.

"Anyhow, if you insist," Lia said pensively, "the teeth in the nurse's cunt were sharp and voracious, and every so often they'd gnash open and shut, all set to shred you—"

"What about the green forked tongue?" Sid interrupted her. Why had he got stuck on that one detail? What had gotten into him? He had no idea.

Lia stared at him vacantly.

"What about the green forked tongue?" he repeated, and became aware that his voice was trembling.

He looked away. The old lady was now awake, and trying to sit up in bed. Sid glanced in the direction of the door to see if her nurse was still there.

"Remember the cod-liver oil?" Lia asked. "Remember Marigoula, the maid who kept an eye on us to make sure we didn't spit it out? Childhood—what a load of misery! The wretched age—"

"—while Dad would be waiting in the dining room and give each of us a chunk of orange peel afterward," Sid said.

"Waiter!" the old lady suddenly screamed.

"You're wanted," said Lia.

Sid stared at her in astonishment.

"Don't worry about it," Lia said, laughing. "Her nurse'll be right back."

"What made you think of Marigoula?" Sid asked.

"Don't you remember the way she'd spy on us, and the kick she got out of telling? And that time she scratched her arm with a pin and ran crying to Mom and said you'd hit her?"

"Waiter! Waiter! Get the chambermaid for me!"

The old lady was definitely addressing Sid. He went to the door and took a look outside. The nurse was nowhere to be seen. He came back and sat down at the foot of the bed with his back turned toward the patient.

Lia sighed. "And after that little episode, don't you remember how Mom told Dad, as usual, and Dad blew his top, and chased you to give you a spanking, but couldn't catch you, and threw a bucketful of water over you from up on the terrace, and I accidentally got in his way when he was after you, and he gave me such a wallop that it knocked me down and made my head go round—"

"That never happened," Sid said placidly. He glanced quickly over his shoulder to see what the old lady was up to.

"It did so happen," Lia insisted, "and one day you hung upside down out of the bathroom window over a high drop, with a real risk of falling and killing yourself, just to get a private peep into Marigoula's room, and you caught her redhanded in the act of making scratches on her hands with a big needle—"

Why do you make me the protagonist in these scenarios of yours? Why do you always want to distort the truth? Sid wondered, but didn't say. "I'd forgotten all that," he said, humoring her.

"All that to tell you that Marigoula was a stunning piece of goods," Lia said, with sudden excitement. "And she wore black garters like the nurse—"

"Waiter!" the old lady cut in.

Sid turned toward her.

"Stand up straight when you talk," she told him.

Sid got to his feet, abashed.

"I want my afternon tea tray," she announced imperiously, and turned to Lia. "The service here is a disgrace, I shall complain to the manager—"

"You're absolutely right," Lia agreed. "On your way, waiter," she told Sid.

Sid went into the corridor in search of the nurse. She was sitting out on the terrace, smoking. The minute she saw him coming she flipped her cigarette over the balustrade and hurried inside without saying a word to him. Sid followed her back to the ward, shutting the terrace doors behind him.

Lia had collapsed again: in the few moments he had been gone her condition seemed to have worsened. Her head was slumped back on the pillow, listless, separate from her body. Her eyes stared glassily into the void. Sid placed one hand gently on her forehead: it was dry and hot. "You got a fever again?" he asked.

"*Hcnvmb*, that's what I've got," she whispered.

"I don't understand," Sid said awkwardly.

"What's Kalotychos been saying to you, so that now you don't understand?" Her tone was sarcastic, but he looked so terrified that she didn't go on. "Better just forget it," she said. "It's not something I'm really concerned about. And anyway—" She eyed him mockingly.

Sid tried to detach his gaze from hers. "And anyway, what?" he asked.

"What...What..." Lia said dully. She turned her face to the wall and didn't speak again.

Useless, helpless. Useless, that's what he felt. Useless, helpless, scared. He looked out the window. This sluggish day wasn't making any progress at all. The light was dazzling. From some unknown point the sun was scorching the earth. The stillness was absolute, and yet... the diaphanous air was sending out crystalline sounds he couldn't hear.

In the dreadful calm the old lady began grousing again. "Send for the manager," she told the nurse. "This hotel is a scandal."

The nurse pulled a face and didn't answer.

"Pack my bags. I want to leave this place. And tell the manager to come here immediately, and to bring the safe-deposit box with my jewelry. Quick march! Didn't yo understand what I told yo? What are yo staring at me like that for? Much better for us to go back to the Côte d'Azur, back to Monte Carlo—"

Lia, who had turned to observe this scene, now brought her attention back to Sid, and spoke to him in a quiet, serious voice.

"Look, I know what the others say about me here, but it isn't true."

Sid waited. The air suddenly seemed to thicken around him. For a split second he felt difficulty in listening to her and breathing at the same time.

"They're wrong, I'm not an eccentric—you know that, don't you? It's just that I can't bear anyone else sleeping in the same room with me. Not even a puppy. Not even a gnat. At night I hear this other creature breathing, and its rhythm is totally different from mine—just listening to it makes me feel like I'm being asphyxiated—"

A nurse entered the ward, and Lia stopped talking. The woman came over to her bed and checked the flow of the I.V. drip. "Anything you need?" she asked. Lia shook her head.

"I'll have a word with the head nurse," Sid said, as soon as the nurse had gone.

"No, don't," Lia said, and hurriedly added: "You've got to leave right away, the Prize Student's shift is just beginning."

She lied to me, Sid thought. He was walking through the hospital's courtyard, beside the dried-up bitter-orange trees. The ground was littered with fallen oranges, split open and rotting. Without actually knowing it he was sure that Sotiris didn't in fact have a shift that afternoon. And why didn't I react? he asked himself. Why didn't I tell her I knew she wanted to get rid of me? Useless, senseless coward. Coward. That's why she can't stand my presence. Because I sit there staring at her with a wishy-washy look on my face. Because I'm more scared than she is.

Two hours later, standing inside at the bar, Sid was drinking his second whiskey, leaning back against the counter. When he got to the Banana Moon he'd sought refuge in the back lounge, where no one went in summer. Here, in the cool half-light, he tried to get his thoughts in order. Beginning, middle, end. Cause and effect. That was what he needed now. That was how a human being had to think. His mind was vacant, drained of even a dribble of logic. He had to get to the bottom of things. He couldn't. As he worked through his third whiskey, Kalotychos's words took on a poetic dimension. So poetic that they almost canceled out the strong smell of his breath and the trembling of his hands. He found a bowl of pistachios and munched a handful of them. The Don Quixote virus. No, wrong. The virus devoured one's organs, ripped them to bits. It was the body that was Don Quixote. Besides, the virus didn't exist. What's more, the problem was one of feelings, not thoughts. And when it came to feelings, he was totally useless. As always, things were happening at the wrong time, to the wrong person. And he was getting out of focus, coming apart.

The day was over. A new barman appeared, and started his shift with a falsely happy air. The spotlights in the trees were switched on. As it grew dark, people began to gather, various young men with tans and white pants were drawn, magnetized, into the wasps' nest. Someone who looked like P., or perhaps actually was P., went by on the sidewalk. A bit absent-minded, blasé, hunched into a lifestyle of his own. Sid pretended not to see him. He'd begun to feel a slight discomfort as he watched the regulars slowly forming into groups and filling the tables under the mulberry trees. From where he stood he could see the faces of these strangers as they advanced, wavering in a state of fragile excitement, each choosing a place and staking out his presence there.

He had paid and was about to leave when he saw her passing on the sidewalk. Her face was bright under the illuminated mulberry trees. For an instant she was the Wingless Victory, with pale unruly breasts gleaming from a square-cut décolleté dress.

"Sid!" she called, without making any move toward him, "are you OK?"

He shook his head.

The girl looked at him frowning and stood, hesitating in the doorway. She looked quickly behind her, and decided to come inside to him. As she made her way through the inside of the bar, zigzag between the empty tables, her face darkened, became clouded, heavy, and suddenly aged. He'd never before noticed the lines on her forehead.

"Aren't you going away on vacation?" she asked him, shaking the hair back off her face.

"I'm always on vacation," he replied, and at once regretted the remark.

The girl looked at him with a troubled smile. So many wrinkles on that cool forehead. Why? he wondered. Julia, what's happening to you?

She spoke to him in vague terms about some summer seminar run by her school that she'd decided to attend. But he couldn't concentrate on what she was telling him. For an instant he felt a strong impulse to ask her to go home with him, to watch some idiot show on TV, to talk to her about Lia. But the invitation remained unspoken. He told her he was tired, and left her there staring after him in bewilderment, still with a smile on her aging face, while he walked away as fast as he could, trying to keep his gait steady. End.

"Now I'm invulnerable," Lia said in her solitude, and gave a hoarse laugh. During the night her condition had worsened. Her body was hooked up to a respirator, several I.V. drips, and various lengths of tubing, making her look like an octopus.

Early in the morning an unexpected improvement took place. The head nurse had come into the ward in person, annihilating distance in her lightweight pattens. She'd smiled at Lia and unhooked her from the machine. "We won't be needing this any more," she told her, with an encouraging gesture. So? Everything under control. Wasn't that Sid's favorite phrase?

· 14 ·

Sotiris marched resolutely into Ward 11 that morning. With it or on it, he told himself.* What was fated would happen. He'd been away from the hospital for a week, and in that time his life had been turned completely upside down. The night before he'd been so tormented with worries that he hadn't slept a wink. He had a nasty premonition, which the mynah bird sensed, and stayed awake with him. What was fated would happen, he reflected once more, trying to strengthen his will. Today was his first day back at work, and he had a whole slew of chores that needed to be taken care of. Everything had to be in perfect order and running like clockwork for the visit of the students from the Physicians' Assistants School.

* This Doric aphorism, still in use, goes back to the ancient world. Spartan wives and mothers told their husbands or sons, as they departed for battle, to "come back either with their shields or on them." *Trans.*

"Good morning," the new nurse said to him. She looked worn out. Beside her the crone was snoring blissfully, her head sunk in lace-trimmed pillows she'd brought from her own home. She was a real screwball, he'd heard all about her already.

The third bed next to the wall looked empty. The halfwit had become invisible, there was just her arm hanging out from the sheet like a branch, hooked up to the I.V. drip. Her condition had deteriorated: most of the time now she spent in a deep torpor. This was the news his colleagues had greeted him with. Well, Sotiris thought to himself, let's get rid of you soon. He chose a sterilized thermometer from the tumbler filled with alcohol and gave it to the private nurse. So far so good, he thought, and proceeded to subject the most inaccessible corners of the ward to a searching and critical scrutiny. The corners that might escape his attention. He took the temperature chart from the bottom of the bed and studied the old lady's fever graph with an air of profundity. "We're doing fine," he said, nodding his head. The nurse gave him an icy glance as though she couldn't care less.

"Bring me that *boteille*," Lia heard the old lady shout. She tried to get herself properly awake, but sleep pulled her under again. Her limbs were numb, and a sweet languor was surging through her now in cycles, lying heavy on her wrists where the blood trickled through drop by slow drop.

"What?" The acid voice of the private nurse sliced through the room.

"The *boteille de cologne*," said her patient, sighing in irritation.

For a little while, perhaps only a matter of minutes, it was quiet. Shadows with vast black wings grew and spread in her mind, drawing her back into another dream, in a room with no corners or walls, itself lost in some earlier dream colored like a green onion. Without wanting to, Lia was sinking into the next sleep, which seemed less like sleep than weakness, a kind of protracted hangover. A brightly lit skylight was in her line of vision, but the hangover interposed itself like a screen and stopped her from looking through it.

"I want the spon."

Silence. Someone gets up, takes a couple of steps, hunts around for something. And sits back down.

"Not that one!"

"Which, then?"

"The sop spon!" the old lady screeched.

"What?" The voice sounded like a sob.

Zocchini, Lia thought, staring, eyes shut, at the bright skylight. Spon. Zocchini. The word had been going round in her head all night, had been with her ever since dinnertime. "Zocchini again?" the old lady had complained, on seeing the tray her nurse brought her. It was an oddity, a minor failure that Lia found herself thinking about when she was hooked up to the respirator. Something almost imperceptible, that she'd noticed over the past few days, now began to make sense. *Boteille*, spon, zocchini, sop. That was it, that explained everything. The old lady had eliminated the *ou* sound from her speech. Did she find it coarse? Vulgar? Lia was too drained to think clearly.

"What? Whaaaat?" The nurse's voice rasped in her larynx.

"Oh, give the woman her soup spoon," Lia said. She'd mustered all her strength to get herself awake, and her words were choked off by a wild fit of coughing.

Hey look, thought Sotiris in astonishment, the corpse is talking.

"Where can I find some aspirin?" The plump private nurse cut in on his thoughts. She had come up very close and was rubbing her hands on her uniform. Dark rings made circles around her eyes. "My head feels like it's about to split," she whispered. Sotiris felt in his pockets. He was prepared for everything. "Take two of these," he said to the girl, with a wave of his hand to indicate that thanks were unnecessary. The nurse went straight over to the washbasin, buttocks shimmying under the tight cloth of her gown, turned on the faucet, filled a plastic cup to the brim, stuck the pills on her tongue and swallowed them in a single gulp.

"If I stay here another day I'll go out of my mind," she said, without looking at him, as she went by. That's life, sweetheart, he wanted to tell her. That's how things are. Sink or swim. This kind of incident didn't upset Sotiris. What had upset him, very considerably, was the sight of the nurse's tongue.

Thick and fat, with deep grooves in it, like cracked earth in summer. A very different, meaty tongue, not like the halfwit's, which would be small and pointed—if she opened her mouth, out would pop a viper's tongue, dripping poison and hissing. Her head had become even smaller than St. Andrew's skull.* She's going to kick off any minute, he thought again. And yet—in a few short moments the corpse had recovered from her fit of coughing, which wasn't in fact a cough but a fine old bronchial spasm—you didn't need to be a doctor to realize that—and had sat up in bed.

"Have a nice vacation?" she asked him abruptly. Despite the state she was in, she gave him an ironic look.

"Great, great," he mumbled hurriedly, and made for the door. Better to restrain oneself. Better not to pay attention to her.

He stopped at the door, and waited. He wondered if she'd spoken to Kalotychos, if she'd reported him over the incident in the doctors' office. Maybe not yet. Maybe she wanted to torment him first, to roast him slowly over a low fire. People at death's door get to be like the Lernaean Hydra.† It'd have been better if he'd clouted her a couple more times that day, finished her off properly, smashed her face in. At least he'd have got a kick out of that.

---

*A famous relic, paraded through the streets of Patras, where St. Andrew had been crucified, and where Sotiris might well have seen it, on the saint's name day. *Trans.*

† The Hydra, in Greek mythology, was a monstrous many-headed water snake, dwelling in a swamp at Lerna in the Peloponnese. For every head cut off, two more grew back (this is what Sotiris has in mind). The monster was finally disposed of by Herakles as one of his Labors. *Trans.*

A group was approaching from the far end of the corridor, laughing and chatting. Three men, and the rest of them girls, in backless dresses with shoulder straps, and platform sandals. There were about ten of them all told, and they looked like people on their way to a party. When they got to where he stood, a man of about thirty detached himself from the group, took a step or two forward, and addressed Sotiris. "This Ward 11?"

Sotiris nodded.

"We're from the Physicians' Assistants School," the group leader announced in a cheery voice.

"I know that," Sotiris cut in. "But it's still too early, you'll have to wait outside—" Firmness and politeness. For some reason his response satisfied him. He noted that the group quieted down and became somehow more compliant. Firmness, politeness, and something else... Precision, he thought, as he watched the group leader go back and explain the position to the others, who heard him out with visible boredom. Precision, that was the thing. Kalotychos would be proud of me. Sotiris went over in his mind the Professor's instructions for visits to the hospital by students.

Ah, at last! The team of doctors appeared at the other end of the corridor, in front of the office, and stood waiting in a small circle. The bathroom door opened and shut. One doctor clapped another amiably on the shoulder. Kalotychos came briskly out, and they all moved off behind him.

"I'm assuming that your visit here is to a certain extent as, h'm, tourists," Kalotychos said, getting straight to the point. Sotiris went and stood behind the doctors to get a good look at the group. "In any case, I think it will help you, regardless, to observe the procedure during doctors' rounds at a university hospital. To understand what a doctor expects of you, and what assistance you can render to him. Do I make myself clear?" he asked, and moved quickly over to the halfwit's bed. No one's following what he's saying, Sotiris realized. Not even the group leader. Only one girl was taking notes, and she was chewing gum. A thin chick who looked a bit like a monkey, dressed in punk clothes.

Kalotychos put his hand on the corpse's shoulder. "I hear you had a difficult night—" he told her. He gave a quick glance at the flow in the I.V. tube.

"I had a hell of a time," said the halfwit. Her expression was bitter.

Kalotychos eyed her sadly, gave her an affectionate pat, and removed his hand from her shoulder. "As I've stressed on other occasions, the fundamental principle here is full cooperation with colleagues in other disciplines. Particularly as regards difficult cases. Medicine isn't just a crucial service, it's an entire philosophy. No one can any longer maintain that a surgical operation suffices to eradicate the pathological root of a problem—"

"If your head hurts, chop it off," said someone in the group, and guffawed.

"Precisely," Kalotychos said, with no sign of irritation. "Every day we come up against real enigmas, difficult cases the progress of which can falsify all our previous experience, call into question established treatments—"

"Why don't you talk to them about *Hcnvmb*?" the halfwit broke in.

What's got into her? Sotiris wondered. What's it going to be this time? Playing the doctor?

"—and that," Kalotychos continued, calmly, "is why I suggest to you—"

"I think *Hcnvmb* is the best possible example of this problem, and the students will find it very exciting," said the halfwit, interrupting again.

"I don't think so," Kalotychos responded calmly.

She's over the edge, Sotiris thought, she's had it. *Troubles never come singly.* That was his father's favorite proverb before he got stuck on *Leave sheep to shepherds.*

"The essential thing is precision: precision, circumspection, and no hasty conclusions."

Precision. We think along identical lines, Sotiris told himself, and felt slightly euphoric. Now he could relax and look the girls over at his leisure. The one with the wad of gum, taking notes, was quite attractive. And she was paying attention to the Professor's words, she didn't miss a thing. She had a wild hair-do that made her look as if the wind had blown her hair all over the place, as if a tornado had snatched her up and then suddenly dumped her. At that moment the girl glanced around to see if anyone was watching her, then spat her gum out into her hand and stuck it behind one ear. A little pink tongue like a sugar almond. Sotiris just caught a glimpse of the tip of this tongue, and felt an indefinable sensation: his ears got hot, his throat burned, and he found himself swallowing. Stop that, he told himself, stop it, this isn't the time for that kind of thing. But as she bent over her notes again, her eyes met his.

She smiled at me. Sheee-smiled-at-meeee! Sotiris repeated to himself an hour later. He was pacing to and fro in the head nurse's office, consumed with excitement. For no reason. He felt an urge to do backflips. To jump up and go perform a wild country dance in the corridor. Why? Just because. Because he felt like it. Didn't he too have the right to do as he wanted? To fill the bedpans with wine and offer them around, to make everyone drink from them? Hey, I'm losing it, I've gone nuts, round the bend. She smiled at me, two little rodent's teeth and a tiny pink tongue—His heart was near to bursting. Then he saw the light blinking on the switchboard. Someone wanted him in Ward 11. Reluctantly he went to see what was going on.

"I'm going to throw up," the halfwit whispered as soon as he came in.

Sotiris stopped a couple of yards from the bed and stared at her.

"Well, do something," she said. "Move—"

The crone was awake and muttered something unintelligible. The private nurse was standing there with the bedpan in her hand. She gave a sympathetic nod in his direction and went out of the ward.

"Move, you idiot—"

You're not going to ruin everything for me, Sotiris thought. I won't let you. He approached the bed. The woman's body was convulsed with spasms, strange noises were coming out of it. Stubborn little weasel. There's nothing wrong with you. It's your own nastiness makes you sick. He wanted to throttle her. The halfwit had begun to spit up. "Idiot," she hissed through clenched teeth. "Asshole—" Sotiris fell on her. His mind had gone blank. He was in the grip of the same agitation he'd felt earlier with the student. Why, he could even give her—Because, hey, the corpse had a rack, she had tits!

"Hold it right there!" someone exclaimed, and forcibly hauled him off her. Sotiris shook himself free, panting. He saw the head nurse, together with a nurse he didn't know, from some other department. "May I inquire what's going on here?" Sotiris was shaking all over. They'd caught him on the bed, astride the corpse. "I—I don't know," he stammered.

"Water," the halfwit said, breathlessly.

"When yo don't need them," the crone observed, "that's when all the waiters show up."

"Excuse me?" The head nurse stared, in astonishment, first at the crone, then at her private nurse. Then she turned back to Sotiris. "You stay here," she said, and sent the other nurse to fetch a blood-pressure monitor.

"I just had a crisis, don't get all worked up," the halfwit said. Suddenly she'd come round. She got her water off the nightstand and took a couple of mouthfuls straight from the bottle. "He was trying to get hold of my tongue so I wouldn't bite it." Her eyes were fixed on the sheet. She'd covered for him. She'd saved him. For what reason? What did she want from him, what was she after? Because she was after something, that was for sure.

"If yo've all come here after tips," sniggered the crone behind his back, "yo're wasting yoh time."

The head nurse looked at Sotiris in disbelief. "If this happens again, I'll report you," she said to him privately as he was about to leave. But she didn't seem angry.

I had a bad premonition. That's why I was up all night. I had a bad premonition, but everything went OK, Sotiris thought as he walked out of the hospital, trying to reassure himself. He was still badly shaken up. He kicked a bitter orange, and watched it come apart as it rolled along the ground, like a disintegrating meatball. The incident in the ward, his jumping astride the corpse, his panting breath, the struggle—all this now seemed unreal to him, a lie, a bad dream. Who could ever have imagined it? The corpse had tits. Small, but fully rounded. He recalled how they stood out from the bones of her ribcage, and his palms began to tingle. He couldn't cope with the fact that he'd acted so crazily. How did I ever blow it like that? Losing control that way—and in the hospital! He'd managed to scare himself, he realized that now. Maybe none of it really happened, he thought. Maybe someone bewitched me. Such goings-on were really too unlikely. He glanced back at the bitter orange, now nestling in the trench they'd dug to create a wheelchair crossing. The work had been going on all summer and getting nowhere. It just dragged on and on.

"Hi there."

"Hi." Sotiris rubbed the back of his neck in embarrassment.

"Phew! They took us all round the hospital like we were tourists, I got really pissed off. No, actually, not so much pissed off as bored. I got bored, so I walked out. Oh, it's so hot, I don't know what I'm saying—" She looked at him, eyes half-shut because she had the sun in her face.

"Yeah, I understand," he said.

"What's your name?" She smiled at him, showing her tiny teeth.

"Sotiris."

"Hi. I'm Julia." Her little tongue had gone under cover and wasn't visible.

"Nice to meet you."

That easy?
That easy.

· 15 ·

*T*wo days after her run-in with the nurse, Lia got her period. She felt something sticking to her bony thighs, something warm dripping between them, and then a sweetish, faintly sour odor spreading from the sheets. There was a bloodstain on her nightgown. How long had it been since the last time? she wondered. She couldn't recall. For a little while she lay quite still, till she could single out that particular mild ache, isolate it from the others that plagued her body, be inundated by a wonderful feeling of sweet sickness in the groin. She remembered how much she used to enjoy the smell of her period. When she was young she would stick her finger in deep and smell it, finally lick it. This gave her a huge thrill, she imagined that at any moment she was going to faint. She would shut herself in her room, with the lights off; she could spend hours in that languorous state.

Some unknown god or demon must have remembered that I'm a woman, she thought, as she dragged herself, with desperate effort, to the bathroom. She wanted to be alone, to change her panties, and wash out the dirty ones in total undisturbed peace. She closed the door behind her, leaned on the sink, and looked at her reflection. Her eyes were sunken, her vision blurred. Her watery image stared back at her from the mirror, like someone's face glimpsed through a rain swept window. Her skin was dotted with raindrops. She tried to wipe the mirror clear with her hand. Nothing changed. Her face was all bedewed. Her lips opened and shut, then parted a little and remained open. She got closer to the mirror and inspected herself. She tried again. No good: she couldn't shut her mouth.

Her face wore a set expression of anticipation. The corners of her mouth, the angle of her nose, her chin, were trapped. She tried to make a few faces. Nothing happened. The expression remained unaltered. Her face was waiting, held captive. When did this happen to me? How long ago? Her body trembled, she felt as though she was losing her balance. She leaned against the sink and looked at her bare legs. A thin rivulet of blood was now trickling all the way down her calf. She turned her gaze back to the mirror. Her lips were half parted, in expectation. What's my mouth waiting for? What am I waiting for? Lots of little kisses, she thought suddenly, that's what

I always enjoyed. Little kisses, non-stop. She pressed her face to the mirror and kissed herself on the lips. *Thud. Thud.* All she could hear was the sound of her heart going *thud thud* inside its empty shell.

Now she remembered. It was one winter a few years back. A rainy day. They'd met accidentally outside a drycleaner's. No. Their meeting wasn't accidental, they'd run into each other again after a long time. Whatever. She was clutching a bag full of dirty laundry, and he had something on a hanger, a jacket maybe. They'd embraced under the tin roof, with the rain dripping off it. They began kissing, and went on till their lips bled. She'd forgotten who the man was, and anyway he didn't particularly interest her. Yet for several evenings she'd kept the taste of those kisses in her mouth. Greedy, devouring kisses, with a tongue gone wild and teeth ready. Something else now, a salty mist—when was that? That was a different man, with a round, girlish mouth. She felt like she was kissing her brother, but it didn't bother her. This guy kissed clumsily, his lips slightly constricted, as though he was trying to protect his gums. Lots of clumsy, urgent kisses. Countless little kisses. And the salty mist? That was someone else again, someone middle-aged. She couldn't be certain now, but when she was fondling his head there had been this inexplicable sensation in the palms of her hands, because on his pate he had just fuzz, and his hair was laid across that like a turban from one ear to the other. He'd flirted with her in the dining room and finally caught her on the bridge. He was the ship's purser. They'd started kissing on the deck, with her back bumping up against a lifeboat. She didn't find this guy at all attractive, she was almost actively disgusted by his body, but she adored his kisses— sweet, rather unctuous, with an abundance of saliva and a tongue as thick and supple as a snake, leaving the taste of Turkish coffee and heavy, sweet red wine deep in her mouth. His hands were busy exploring her body, but she wouldn't let him go any further, it was the kisses she couldn't get enough of, she wanted more kisses, nothing but his kisses, she felt she could come just from that, or maybe she'd already had a whole succession of orgasms. At some point he got mad and took off. But just as he was going, highly upset, a sea breeze uncovered his bald crown, and the strands of hair that had come unstuck stood straight up like a lacquered prick. She'd stayed there for hours, she'd spent the night leaning against the taffrail, licking her lips, inhaling the salt sea mist.

She took a step back from the mirror and stood stock-still. She could no longer hear her heartbeat, only a faint buzzing in her ears. With one hand clutching the faucet she changed her panties. Holding the dirty pair in her other hand, she leaned across the sink and wiped the mirror. The mark left behind by the blood was brownish, not red. Through this brownish blur she looked at herself again. Her lips were still half parted. Still wore the same fixed expression. Thirsty for kisses. Mmmm—no, not like that. No. Bloodsucking kisses weren't her thing at all. Nor were jackhammer tongues. Gentler, softer, slower—that's the way. Now quicker. Tiny bites. Lots of tiny kisses and every so often a barely noticeable nip at the tip of the tongue. Harder, harder! Bite me, I mean it, bite me! Again. And again—like that. Now softer again. Easy does it. Don't go too fast... Stop! Now we're going to start all over again, right from the beginning... My lips don't press on yours, they barely make contact, they rest on yours, as if they wanted to get to know you from scratch. You're crying. Why are you crying? I'm just crazy about kisses with tears. Saliva and tears all mixed up. I want more. Don't be scared. More! Why are you stopping? What's got into you to make you stop now? Kiss me, kiss me. Tear out my tongue. Swallow my lips, suck out my eyes, do it! Now take me, take me! Rip me apart, now! I'm tired, get out. Get out. I'm sick of this. Let me be. Come here. Come here! We'll start over from the beginning—

"Bro—"
"Huh?"
"Bro, it's me, open up!"
"I'll be out in a minute."
"You all right?"
"Yes."
"Sure?"
"Yes."

"I've got a surprise for you."
"What's happened?"
"I found a job. Starting in September."
They had gone out onto the terrace for a little, but Lia tired quickly, and they went back inside.
"Bravo! Congratulations!"
"Don't you make fun of me."

"How much are they going to pay you?"

"I'm thinking of resigning."

"Don't be an idiot."

"They took me on for some committee to do with the Olympic games. I'll be sending out press announcements by fax—"

"And maybe you'll meet one of those knockout chicks with a morocco organizer and a leather garter belt."

"Yeah, maybe. I've put on five pounds."

"Doesn't matter, you look great."

"No woman's interested in me."

"You're not interested in any woman."

Sid grinned. He laid his hand lightly on her arm, and kept it there. Five, ten minutes went by. His fingers began to press into her skin. Poor Sid. This role doesn't suit you at all. The brother, the guardian angel. We're face to face, and you don't even dare meet my eye. A committee for the Olympic Games—couldn't you have come up with something a bit more impressive than that? You can't even think of a joke. She took his hand from her arm, and held it between her own.

"Can you believe I got my period? Can you believe that?" Tears lurked in her eyes, stinging them.

"So what?" Sid shrugged his shoulders, unimpressed. "The way you announce it, at the very least you should have grown a beard."

"Please—" Lia whispered. She pulled her hands away, and Sid's hand dropped on the sheet.

"Unless I'm much mistaken, women do have

periods. Oh yes, and cats do, too. Hey, what's up with you? Have you gone crazy? You're crying—"

"Leave me alone."

"Don't cry, please don't—"

"All right, it's over." She wiped away her tears with a corner of the sheet.

"Don't cry, I'll take you out of here."

"All right."

"Don't cry, everything'll be fine."

"Everything'll be fine, I promise you." That was what Sid had told her, and then he'd taken off like a man on the run. I promise you. I promise you. Everything is under control. That was what Sid believed. That was what he wanted to believe. From bad to worse. Most of the time she had a high temperature and was sunk in torpid sleep. It wasn't all that terrible, it was a little like being high—she'd always suspected it might be. She seldom felt any pain, but when she did it was unbearable. Like a fingernail thrust into her brain.

· 16 ·

A studio apartment is a studio apartment. It can't be transformed into a Beverly Hills suite. Miracles don't happen, Sotiris thought, running a duster for the umpteenth time over the television set. As the time for his date drew near he was panic-stricken, scared that he wouldn't be up to the occasion. This was the first time a girl was visiting him at home—and what a girl! Both educated and modern. Mama Koula wouldn't believe her eyes if she saw her. Good-looking? Yeah, good-looking, but in an odd way. At one point he thought of calling Thanási to get some advice. Better not, he decided. In case he makes a mess of things again, the way he did in the village. "And you sit tight," he warned the mynah. "Don't you go ruining my plans."

He showered, dried himself, dabbed on some cologne, and settled down, naked, in front of the television, to avoid sweating and having his armpits smell. Things had worked out far more easily than he'd imagined. After their encounter in the hospital courtyard, they'd walked together to the bus stop and caught the same bus. What had they talked about? He was in such a nervous state he couldn't remember. Anyway she'd done most of the talking— about her school, and the friends she had there. And finally, just before she got off the bus, it was she who, unprompted, had suggested meeting again. Followed by a brisk farewell "Ciao!" from the sidewalk while he'd been left in a daze, waving to her.

When the telephone rang, he was absolutely convinced it had to be her calling to cancel their date.

"I'm really down in the dumps—" It was Thanási's voice.

"What's been happening?"

"Big troubles—can't really tell you over the phone—"

Sotiris glanced anxiously at his alarm clock. It was nearly time, and he was still stark naked.

"—so let's go to a taverna and talk things over—" Thanási was saying.

"Yeah, let's make a date for that."

"What's the matter with you?" Thanási sounded worried.

"Nothing, it's just that I can't make it today."

"But we're friends, aren't we?"

"I can't make it today, I'm telling you straight out," said Sotiris evenly.

"OK, fine." A pause. "How's the mynah doing?"
"How do you think? She's fine, just fine."

Was I too sharp with him, Sotiris wondered as he opened his closet. Did I cut him off too abruptly? He grabbed the can of talc and generously dusted his thighs and member. His sweating bothered him, really got on his nerves. Who knows what may happen today? Who can tell how the evening will turn out? He rubbed in talcum powder, his mind on Julia's mouth and cute little teeth. "Hey, you there," he said to his member, which till then had been curled up and was now getting aroused. "Stop that. No one was talking about you." He got hold of it and pushed it roughly inside his underwear. Then, while he was putting his pants on, twinges of conscience began to assail him again. Thanási had sounded desperate. The guy was too sensitive for his own good, somebody had to take him in hand. Somebody, meaning him. He was Thanási's only friend.

Remorse or no remorse, everything else was forgotten when he saw her walk into his apartment. He opened the door and she marched straight in, no embarrassment or uncomfortable hesitation, just as if it were her own house. She was wearing tight black pants and a close-fitting black blouse, and her hair looked rather more black to him this time, with a reddish lock falling over her forehead and hiding one eye.

It would have been better to call Thanási and ask his advice. Five minutes had gone by with them sitting facing each other, she in the one armchair, he on a chair. He stared at his feet, feeling embarrassed, suddenly aware of an oil stain on one leg of his pants.

"Do you get MTV?" she asked him suddenly.

Sotiris looked at her in surprise.

"Let's see," Julia said. She picked up the remote control from the coffee table, turned on the television, and started surfing channels. "Ah, here it is," she said, satisfied, and flopped back in the armchair. The crotch of her pants had ridden up an inch or two and was cutting into her. She worked the cloth down with two fingers and settled down once more.

She's really thin, Sotiris thought. Now that she was absorbed in the TV program he could study her at his leisure. Her breasts were small and pointed, like inverted cones. Under her thick hair her face was childlike and shy, with a mournful expression. The one thing that really got his attention was her mouth: those small protruding lips, the little pink tongue.

"Aren't you interested in the Top Ten?" She'd turned toward him.

"I only watch the news," he lied.

She raised her eyebrows. "Oh, a culture freak, got it," she said, and gave him a vague smile.

"Hi there, Maria," squawked the mynah. God alone knows how it had gotten shut in the bathroom.

Julia's mouth dropped open. "I don't believe it!" she said.

"It's just a bird, don't be scared," Sotiris reassured her and stood up.

"I just can't believe it!" Julia said again. She

spread her arms wide and slumped back against the headrest of the armchair as though thunderstruck.

"Don't be scared," Sotiris repeated, standing there. Then he opened the bathroom door and switched on the light. The mynah was perched on the toothbrush mug, admiring its reflection in the mirror. From Sotiris's position it looked as though there were two birds in there. He left the door open and came back.

"She'll come out when she wants to, she's obstinate," he told Julia.

"My life's full of weird coincidences," she said, thoughtfully. She looked him in the eye but didn't go on.

Did I mess up somehow? Sotiris wondered. Could she be allergic to birds? Does that mean the end of us? But before he had time to contemplate the various possibilities, he saw the girl get up determinedly and dart into the bathroom. "Maria, it's Julia!" he heard her call out.

"Hi there, Maria," squawked the mynah.

"Ju-li-a!" said Julia.

"Hi there, Maria," the mynah repeated, and flapped its way into the living room. It landed on the television set, and screwed its head round to scratch the back of its neck with its beak.

"I'm going to tell you something," Julia said, leaning toward the lit-up screen, "that I've never told anyone before. I had this relationship, not all that long ago—" She hesitated. "He was a pretty weird guy, made me spit at the singers on TV—"

Sotiris likewise leaned forward, toward her.

"I don't believe it," he said. He shook his head vaguely, wondering if this was the kind of reaction she was expecting from him.

"He'd make me have spitting contests with him."

Sotiris cleared his throat. "Maybe he had psychological problems," he ventured. How'd you ever come up with that one, big guy? he asked himself.

"Now that you mention it—" The girl's expression had become reflective.

We're doing fine, Sotiris thought. He took his courage in both hands and went on: "An immature person—"

"That's it, of course!" The girl's face lit up. "I thought so too, but I was very mixed-up at the time—"

"I understand," Sotiris murmured, wondering what his next move was.

The rest happened very fast. As though a twister had passed through and his life had changed in an instant. He'd offered her Coca-Cola and they'd each drunk two glasses. Then he'd taken Mama Koula's sour cherry out of the fridge. Julia had never tried this before and raved about it.

"I like you because you're different from the others," she told him suddenly.

She stood up. "OK if I go to the bathroom?"

I've had a wretched lonely life, Sotiris thought, watching her move away. How did this ever happen to me? As Julia felt around in the dark for the light switch she stuck out her ass, and something about it reminded him of that young kid with the red shorts, back in the village. But at the moment he didn't want to think about her, she'd brought him nothing but bad luck. Julia was something else again. As long as she doesn't come back out of the bathroom naked. The very idea left him in a cold sweat, it wasn't an appealing prospect at all. Leave sheep to shepherds. The man does the chasing, that's a constant. Anyway the brief moment she was gone didn't give him time to review the situation. The mynah bird had settled down on the television set for a nap. Every so often it would open one eye and give him a worried glance.

"I went to take out my contact lenses, my eyes are smarting," Julia said as she came back into the room.

"Sensible idea," Sotiris whispered, so softly he could scarcely hear his own voice.

For a little while they both remained silent.

"Know something?" she said. "I feel very relaxed with you."

"M-me too," he stammered.

"It's as if I'd known you for years." She had that mournful expression on again.

"And yet there's something bothering you—"

"Yes?" She turned and looked at him, puckering up her round little mouth.

"You look sad."

"I know," she sighed. "I'm always like this." She took the remote control and turned up the volume. "This Prodigy group—just pure depravity."

"The one thing I know is that I know nothing," Sotiris said. Good thing I learned a thing or two from

Thanási. He stretched out his legs and let his muscles relax. He felt great. At this moment nothing could bother him. Not even a grease mark on his pants. Not even if he found himself in trouble at the hospital. What hospital? The hospital didn't exist now. High time he forgot it. It had caused him quite enough bother already. He was going to waste there. Thanási had said so ever since they first met up again, and he was right. At the thought of his classmate he felt even more euphoric. He was a good guy even if he did have his oddities. He, Sotiris, was lucky to have him for a friend. And it didn't matter that he'd turned him down tonight. It was just the one time, and he had a good reason. I'll call him tomorrow, he decided. I'll invite him out to a taverna, my treat.

After the evening news, he got out a couple of beers, made a salad, and cut up a loaf of bread. But what Julia really went for were Mama Koula's stuffed peppers. It was then she told him how she was an orphan, how her mother had died when she was ten years old. A dark shadow passed across her eyes, but luckily she soon regained her cheerful mood. "Is there a thriller on?" she asked him as soon as they'd finished. She'd unzipped her pants and stretched her legs out comfortably on the floor. "Do you think I'm fat?" she asked him coquettishly.

"You're extremely thin," he told her seriously, and from her relaxed and trustful expression he could tell that he'd taken a giant step forward: there was nothing now that could stop him. He glanced at his watch. It was past one o'clock. What had happened today? Why was the guy so late?

The phone rang, and Julia, startled, looked at him. He gestured to her not to worry. "Aren't you going to answer it?" she asked him, on the third ring. Sotiris shook his head. At that moment he felt wonderfully relaxed, and didn't want anything to prise him loose from his delicious state of euphoria.

"Don't tell me!" Julia had sprung to her feet, and flashed him a questioning glance.

"What—?"

"That's the Chinese guy!" she exclaimed, bouncing with excitement.

"How do you know?" Sotiris asked. But she'd already gone and picked up the receiver. She spoke for a moment, then trotted back on her giant platform shoes. Her expression had changed. She knelt at his feet, embraced him, and rested her cheek on his chest. He wanted to stroke her hair but didn't dare to. "How on earth do you know about the Chinese guy?" he asked her, in a husky voice.

"Didn't I tell you my life is full of weird coincidences?" she murmured enigmatically. She stayed like that, clasped close to him, without his daring to touch her.

After a little she said: "I can't think of a crazier place to live in than Athens."

And how is that relevant? Sotiris wondered, but he didn't ask her. He was afraid to. He felt that the slightest thing, even the most commonplace question, might ruin the atmosphere, dissolve that sense of magic that he was experiencing for the first time. Suddenly everything had become so simple. It's now or never, he told himself. And he plunged on.

"Would you like us to get married?" he asked her. He didn't know if the beer had made him drunk or if he'd gone totally nuts.

"That's the second proposal I've had this summer," she said, and lifted herself off him.

"Then you'd better accept it, because there may not be a third," Sotiris said, taken aback by his own coolness.

"Do you by any chance have 'You Are My Destiny'? I'd like to dance."

"You need some sleep," he told her. Good thing he was a nurse. He'd learned how to handle difficult situations, how to avoid pitfalls.

She gave him an odd look, a little scared, but mostly irresolute, and raised no objection. She got up and made straight for the bed. Luckily I changed the sheets, Sotiris thought.

He knew she was taking off her clothes, but he didn't turn to look. When he heard the bed creak under the weight of her body he got up. He switched off the light and opened the window. The moon was not yet full, but it shed enough light into the room.

"Let me just watch you till you fall asleep," he begged.

Julia snuggled close to the wall, and curled herself up. "There'll be a full moon Saturday," she said. Her voice slurred as sleep overtook her. "I like that a lot."

"Me too," Sotiris said, and stroked her hair.

"We can go to the Acropolis and watch it together," she whispered. In a moment her breathing changed, and she was asleep.

All right, Sotiris told himself, we'll watch it together. He took off his shirt and lay down beside her, still in his pants, eyes wide open in the darkness.

· 17 ·

*I*t was a summer out of the blue. The sun rose in the West and was admiring the moon. Words had lost their meaning. Everything went wrong. Everyone said the end of the world was coming. They watched television and wept. A cat announced it was in love with a dog. No one believed it, but they were all mistaken.

Every day I muddled up my thoughts and straightened them out again. Then I put each thought in a separate hiding place around the house. The house began to resemble a mouse trap. Every part of it had its own thought, every piece of furniture was booked, even the sideboard and the fridge. There was no room left for me. I decided to get away from there. I wanted to cut loose from myself and roam around.

It was a weird, scary, ominous, implacable summer. I got ready to leave. Aunt Lela was sitting in front of the television, watching a sitcom and blowing spit bubbles. I felt sorry for her because she looked bored out of her skull. I thought about taking her along with me to rescue her. I went up to her and then I saw she wasn't alone. There was a man sitting beside her, with a gray elephant's trunk. "The boy is mine," she trilled to me...

"What's this nonsense?" Zoe demanded.

"But you didn't read it all," said Nina.

"Why should I? Are you kidding? Papadiamantis you're not—"*

"I don't like Papadiamantis."

"I couldn't care less," said Zoe, with a disagreeable sneer, "but you ought to know that this stuff isn't literature."

"I don't like literature."

"For heavens' sake, how idiotic can you get? If you don't like literature, then why are you doing all this?" Zoe brandished the notebook at her.

"I like writing," Nina said curtly. She was furious, but she didn't want Zoe to know that. She didn't feel upset, just angry. Angry with herself for having been so stupid as to give her notebook to Zoe to read. "Give it back to me. I'm never going to show you anything again."

"I couldn't care less," Zoe said, and put the notebook down on the bench beside her. "Still,

---

* Alexandros Papadiamantis (1851–1911) was a novelist and genre short-story writer from the island of Skiathos, who specialized in nostalgic free association and stream-of-consciousness: hence Zoe's choice of him. *Trans.*

there's one thing I need to tell you. Don't go dragging our aunt into your rubbish any more—"

"Auntie's got nothing to do with it!"

"Oh no? Anyone reading that'll think she spends her time blowing spit bubbles, that she's a retard or something—"

"You don't understand anything," Nina said. "That was a kind of dream."

"No one has dreams like that unless they're—"

"You're a zombie," Nina said. Now I'm absolutely sure, she told herself. She took her notebook, got up, and moved off. She crossed the vacant lot, skirted the distillery, and came out on the main road. She walked along the edge, against the flow of traffic. Her fury had begun to fade away inside her. She stepped down from the sidewalk onto the asphalt. A truck overtook her, with a blast of its horn as it went by. Now I'm a writer. I'm not scared of anything. I hold myself in perfect balance as I advance. From the other direction a jeep was bearing straight down on her. At the last moment the driver swerved to avoid her. He stuck his head out and yelled something. Only I can do this. I'm absolutely alone. I hold myself in perfect balance. That is my shield. She clutched the notebook to her chest.

But the worst thing happened in the evening. They didn't have a lot of customers that day, and by the time the last table emptied it was still early. Mt. Paliovouna was on the point of sinking into the sea. Aunt Lela was emptying the dirty ashtrays into a plastic bag. Zoe had gone up to her and was whispering something to her, with a conspiratorial air.

"What's going on, then?" Mr. Papazoglou asked. Aunt Lela, behind the counter, shook her head but didn't say anything. She went down to the other end of the veranda and stood at the railing beside Nina. She glanced at her once or twice as though waiting for Nina to speak first.

"Why don't you write something nice?" she suddenly asked.

"Something nice?" Nina repeated.

"Yes, well, I don't know—" Aunt Lela mumbled, and paused, thinking. She looked very tired, and her skin was damp and shiny. "Why don't you write about the sunset, or the sea, or your vacation? Yes, that's a good idea, keep a vacation diary, what we do in the shop, how we spend each day—"

"And that's nice?"

Aunt Lela looked at her, expressionless. "I don't know," she said, struggling to make herself clear. "I don't know, but at least it's something true."

Nina remained silent. There was something about Aunt Lela's proposal that she couldn't work out.

"Why don't you write about something real, that's what I mean—"

"I don't know," Nina said. She really meant it, she didn't know. Nor had she ever given it a thought.

"If you don't know, you might as well try," Aunt Lela said, with a touch of impatience. She wiped her hands on her apron and studied Nina out of the corner of one eye. "You might as well try," she repeated, and went back to the counter.

Hours later, Nina suddenly woke in the middle of the night. She thought she'd heard a conversation going on in her sleep, someone persistently calling her name. Beside her Zoe was lying on her back, fast asleep, head thrown back, arms close along her flanks. Nina sat up in bed and scrutinized her. Zoe lay absolutely motionless on her pillow, as though she wasn't breathing. The moonlight streamed in through the shutters and flooded her nightgown, her body had turned to plaster. Nina bent over her and placed a finger under her sister's nostrils. Zoe took a deep breath and sighed. So she's still alive, Nina thought. For one brief moment she'd prayed for her sister's death, had dreamed up the whole terrible drama, the total confusion in the house, she'd seen her parents looking wretched, dressed in black, and amid it all herself, weeping inconsolably. Zoe muttered something incomprehensible and turned her back on her. Nina began to recall the events of the evening just past, what Aunt Lela had said, Zoe's derisive expression when she read her notebook, the mean look she'd had when talking to Aunt Lela, the way Zoe had betrayed her, the whole humiliating business from start to finish. She let her feet slide onto the floor, and got up. Whispers were audible from the veranda. She went to the window and peered through the half-open shutters. Her aunt and Mr. Papazoglou were out there in the dark, arms around each other, talking.

Nina went downstairs very quietly. The kitchen was plunged in darkness. A kind of dirty snowstorm was playing across the TV screen, and she could hear the nonstop crackle of static. Blackie was curled up asleep in front of the refrigerator. "Come on, Blackie, wake up," Nina whispered. She went over and scratched him with her foot. "Come on," she said again. The puppy paid no attention to her.

"I have a serious responsibility," Aunt Lela was saying.

Mr. Papazoglou mumbled something inaudible.

Nina stole to the door and stood there listening.

"She's been getting so strange. I've got to tell her parents."

Again Mr. Papazoglou said something inaudible.

"I can't keep her here any longer." Her voice was sharp, decisive.

"Come here," said Mr. Papazoglou.

"I am here," Aunt Lela said, puzzled.

"Come here," he repeated, in a different tone of voice.

A chair scraped across the floor. Then silence.

Nina retreated a few steps, leaned against the refrigerator, and stood motionless. She tried to hold her breath. It seemed to her that she could distinguish both the noise of the breeze eddying among the willows and, from further off, the monotonous murmur of the sea as it surged in along the shoreline, dragging seaweed with it.

A stinging sound like a slap came from the veranda. Mr. Papazoglou burst out laughing. "Stop that, leave me alone—" That was Aunt Lela, behaving as though someone was tickling her.

Zombies, Nina thought. And they wanted to run her life. Her eyes filled with tears. She tried to stay cool, but couldn't manage it. She turned round, clutched the refrigerator with both hands, and shook it. "Listen, you zombies," she whispered, "I hate you, I hate you—" Outside on the veranda the laughter had grown louder. Write something nice— Write! Rage and fury surged up inside her. Write something true! Write about the sunset! Write! Nina kicked the refrigerator with all her strength. Blackie sprang up in alarm.

· 18 ·

*H*ow are you feeling today?" Sid asked her. He was clutching a bottle of wine, and stood there swaying slightly, as though afraid of losing his balance. "We'll need a bottle opener," he said.

Lia nodded, and closed her eyes.

Sid looked around. The old lady was reclining on a wide lace-edged pillow, and her eyes, wide as saucers, were studying a yellowed snapshot she held in her bony fingers. Beside her, perched on a stool, her nurse was absorbed in a magazine with color pictures, and every so often her lips would move as she followed the text of a caption. A jolt like a subterranean tremor went through the room and set him swaying on his feet again. "Bordeaux, 1965 vintage," he said to himself. He put the bottle on the nightstand and sat down on the edge of the bed.

Something about the quality of the air in the ward had changed, because today everything smelled filthy. Chlorine, medicines, vomit. Formalin, rubbing alcohol. Body odors. His hand felt for Lia's, found it, pressed it tight in his own. It was soft, and clammy. Limp, nerveless, lifeless. And hot, very hot. He closed his eyes and wondered what he felt at that moment, at that very moment. He squeezed her inert hand and sensed the miniscule bones of the palm detaching and crumbling under his fingers. I feel absolutely nothing, he realized, in amazement. Nothing, except the hunger gnawing at his stomach because he hadn't eaten since the evening before.

"Wonderfol times," sighed the old lady, and stroked the surface of the photograph with trembling fingers.

Once again that same underground tremor passed through the ward and made him shiver. There was a kind of muffled whirring sound. Sid looked outside. A giant yellow crane was now in action opposite the window. For a short while it maneuvered jerkily against the clouds, then abruptly lowered itself and came to a dead halt. Somewhere, in some apartment, someone was moving out. The crane angled for its unseen load, then began returning skyward with a slow, tremulous motion.

"Thanks for the wine," Lia said.

"We'll need a bottle opener," Sid repeated. The nurse looked up and smiled at him over her magazine.

"In the kitchen," Lia said.

"Right," said Sid.

There was nobody in the kitchen. Sid searched around the sink and behind the plate rack. He pulled out drawers and looked inside. He opened the refrigerator. On the top shelf, in various stages of decay, a hunk of cheese with a bite taken out of it, two pots of yogurt, and a few slices of baklava on a plastic plate. The rest of the patients' food was sealed in plastic wrap or stored in nylon bags. For a moment the idea floated through his mind of taking something for a quick snack, but shame won out. As he was leaving the kitchen he ran into a skinny young woman in a floral robe.

"Are you looking for something?" she asked him. She was holding a plate with a rice-stuffed tomato in a thick pool of olive oil.

"A bottle opener," he said.

"A bottle opener?"

"Yeah, for wine."

"I don't know about that," the woman said. She looked anxiously at her plate, as though scared that the tomato might take wing and fly off, and hurried into the kitchen.

"I couldn't find one anywhere," Sid said. Lia opened her eyes and shut them again. She touched one hand to her throat.

"Hurting?" Sid asked.

"Yes."

"Badly?"

"No—" She went on gently exploring her throat with the tips of her fingers.

"I'll go take a look," said the nurse, and got up. With a quick glance at the old lady, still absorbed in her photograph, she left the ward.

Outside, night had begun to fall. The crane made a 180-degree turn on its axis, and gave a slight lurch. Two thick wire coils were unwound on the same elevated tackle block, and paid out quickly in opposite directions till they were stretched taut along the central armature. A small cabin swung into view, and stopped there, suspended in the livid sky.

Sid got up off the bed, and took a couple of steps to start his blood moving.

"That was when we osed to go to Lotraki," the old lady announced.*

Sid walked to the window.

"Waiter, come here," she called out to him.

He looked at her questioningly. She sat waiting, the photograph in her hand.

"That's me," she told him.

She was dressed in white, with a white ribbon in her hair. Eighteen, twenty at the most. Sitting in a wicker chair, on a veranda smothered with honeysuckle. Summer. Behind her was a stout man with a moustache, who was leaning on the balustrade and wearing a portentous expression. In the background were two other figures, possibly women, though the photograph was so faded that it was impossible to be certain.

"Happy days," Sid mumbled.

* Loutraki was, and is, a smart spa near Corinth. *Trans.*

"What wod yo know about that?" the woman sighed. "See him?" she added, one shaky finger indicating the man in the snapshot. "Alevriades & Co., a real gentleman." Her eyes were cloudy with nostalgia. "But what wod yo know about that," she repeated, "the way things were in Lotraki then, with the dinner parties..." Her voice gradually faded.

Sid retreated to the window.

"Come back here!" the old lady bellowed at him. She thrust a hand under her mattress, and felt around for a bit, finally pulling out a velvet pouch. After considerable effort she managed to undo its frayed drawstring.

"Here," she said, and reached out her hand toward him.

"I don't—" Sid began. But there was no sense in refusing. "Thank you," he whispered, took the 100-drachma note, and stuffed it into his pocket.

He stood at the window. The crane had finished its stint of work for the day. Its cabin hung there empty, opposite a small translucent cloud. This was the driver's seat. By now the operator would have climbed down, glad to set foot on solid ground again, to have made it through yet another day. He'd have wiped off his sweat, washed his face. Then he'd go off to meet his friends. Or maybe he'd take his assistant out for a beer. They'd pick seats near the window, and down their beers in huge greedy gulps, caressing the ice-cold glasses and gawking at the people passing to and fro outside. Or perhaps the guy would rather take a stroll by himself after work, crossing the square and going past the playground, deaf to the shrieks of the children around him. He'd make for the park, walking on alone under the eucalyptus trees, between the flowerbeds, quietly at ease in the cool stillness, maybe quickening his pace and moving on briskly, without thinking, till he was completely enveloped in darkness.

"I couldn't find one anywhere," said the private nurse, with the air of an embarrassed child.

"It doesn't matter," Sid said.

"It does matter," the old lady said, with an enigmatic smile. "It does."

She paused. "What is it yo're loking for?"

"A bottle opener for wine," said the nurse. She was standing beside her, rearranging her pillows for the umpteenth time.

"Oh, a corkscroh," said the old lady, her vacant expression lighting up. "Send for the manager, I have one in the casket with my jewelry."

The nurse caught Sid's eye, then knelt down in front of the old lady's nightstand and turned the metal doorknob. The little cabinet was overflowing with a varied assortment of objects. She took out an oval box with a purple velvet cover, opened it, and hunted for a moment among the ancient bric-a-brac inside. "Here it is," she said, and produced a rusty old corkscrew with a carved wooden handle.

"Thank yo, Maître," said the old lady.

She's got me mixed up with Kalotychos, Sid thought. He felt like laughing.

"What are yo waiting for?" the old lady asked, watching them. "I don't want to be late for the reception—"

Sid thought he saw Lia stir. He got close to her and bent down over her face. "We found a bottle opener," he said.

The private nurse brought four glasses from the kitchen. Then she stood watching him impatiently as he struggled to get the ancient instrument through the cork. I could be the center of the world at this moment. If I was drunk, I'd believe I was. But he wasn't drunk. He gripped the bottle between his legs, assumed the appropriate stance, and pulled. The bottle opened with a resounding and celebratory pop. Sid sniffed the cork. An excellent vintage. He poured out four glasses and handed them round.

"Your health," said the old lady.

"I'm not really supposed to drink when I'm on duty," simpered the nurse, and raised the glass to her lips.

Sid tried to lift Lia into a sitting position.

"What are we celebrating?" the old lady asked.

"Walporgis Night," said Lia.

"Walpurgis Night," Sid corrected her.

"Walporgis Night!" said the old lady, very loud. Her cheeks had flushed, and she held out her hand with the empty glass for a refill.

Sid held the glass to Lia's lips, and with an effort she managed a couple of sips. The wine began dribbling down her chin.

"I'll tell you what we're celebrating," Lia said, pushing the glass away with one hand. She tried to prop herself up on her elbows. "It's our engagement," she announced, thickly. Her lips were reddened from the wine.

"Cheers," said the old lady, and emptied her glass at one gulp.

Sid felt a hot blush course through his face. He looked first at the nurse, whose eyes were fixed in embarrassment on the dregs in the bottom of her glass, and then at his sister, who had slumped back on her pillows. He tried to assume a carefree expression. "Here's to our engagement!" he said in his turn, and drained his glass.

The nurse stared at him, dumbfounded.

"Just one of my sister's little jokes," he muttered, waving his empty glass in the nurse's direction.

"Propooze—" he suddenly heard Lia call out, in a high squeak. "Let's propooze a toost—"

"Propose a toast?" Sid gave a nervous smile. He was beginning to perspire.

"Poot-latch," Lia mouthed. "Pooplars—"

"Poomegranates?" said Sid uncertainly, trying to encourage her.

"Podles," she whispered, looking straight at him.

For a moment Sid wavered in confusion.

"Poop-coorn?" he mumbled hesitantly. Let her stop here, he prayed in his heart. Let her stop now, this instant.

But Lia didn't stop. "Possy," she said. "Pofters. Podle-fo—" Her words choked on what sounded like hiccups or dry heaves. Then, eyes watery and voice cracking, she doubled right over in front of him.

Panic-stricken, Sid bent down and caught hold of her by the shoulders, raising her up and letting her body slide slowly down and stretch out on the bed. When she was finally in a position to lie back and relax, he knelt down at her side and took hold of her hand. Her pulse was weak, but plainly discernible. Her forehead was burning hot, and beaded with tiny drops of sweat. He wondered what the time was. How late was it? He needed to know. He leaned over the bed and rested his head on her shoulder. Two, three, five minutes, half an hour passed like this. Everything was quiet, very quiet. Outside it was beginning to get dark. There was this gulf between her face and his, this silence spreading through the ward. He gathered Lia into his arms and held her close. Now he could make out her breathing, her pulse still beating. Finally he whispered: "Bro—?"

Her lips stirred. "Don't go," she said. Her voice was faint but cool. Then she sank into a lethargy.

"Ninety-six point two, her temperature's right down." The head nurse delivered her oracle.

"Finally," Sid said. He gave the doctor an encouraging glance. He was still clutching his sister's hand, but now he let his fingers relax their hold. The duty doctor had an evasive expression that Sid didn't like. He was a dark man of about thirty, with untidy hair, who smelled of something like garlic and looked as though he'd just been woken up. His medical gown was unbuttoned. He'll be in a bad mood because we got him out of bed, Sid thought.

"Well, Doctor?" he said, with an attempt at a smile.

The doctor studied him thoughtfully and shook his head. "We're here," he replied, and spread his hands. Then he gestured to the head nurse to follow him, and left the ward.

Somewhere in the distance a church clock struck midnight. Twelve crisp strokes. The lights in the corridor had been turned off for the past hour. In the ward there was just the one dim green night-light. Sid found himself thinking about Sotiris, and the business with Lia, and how the whole thing had begun when the nurse had fixed the electrical system one night so that the lights in the ward where his sister was wouldn't go out. Of course, that was the story the way she told it, he could never be sure. And Sotiris wasn't any kind of monster, just a poor slob. Sid remembered the mynah, maybe missed it a little. When he got home it would have been nice to find it there.

Sid stood up from the bed, went over to the window, and rested his full weight on the sill. The crane's steel backbone gleamed in the light of the rising moon, like the skeleton of some prehistoric animal. The sky was lower now. A star that may have been an airplane blinked past and disappeared. *Here is where life ends*—a forgotten line came to his lips. How did it go? What came next? *The soul like a swallow flies out of my breast.* That was the sort of sentimental song that always sickened him. He felt exhausted; his feet were sore; his muscles, drained of blood, were seizing up. Somewhere in the distance a dog started barking, an endless, drawn-out yowl. Sid stared up at the ceiling. It seemed to be shaking slightly, as though someone was marching heavily across the floor above. For a moment he strained his ears to catch the various sounds. Someone, he thought, was playing the piano. A children's sonatina.

Here is where life ends... it issues from my lips...

Sid tapped several times on the warm windowpane. His fingertips were clammy and trembling. How great it must be out there! How he'd like to get out and go for a stroll, cross the main avenue and make for the park! Further on, in the squares, people would still be about, enjoying the air. By now the heat was sure to have cooled off. The dew would have begun to cover the leaves and branches with its translucent mist, traffic in the streets would have increased, they'd have lit the candles in the open-air restaurants, their flickering illuminating the faces of pretty women. For several moments he remained motionless, thinking about the job he'd be starting in September, the new office, the other employees. Perhaps Lia was right, he might meet a girl, might even embark on some kind of romance.

When he turned back to look inside the ward, the nurse was standing there in the dim light by the door. He couldn't make out her face. All he could see were her feet in their white clogs, which looked freakish in the bluish corpse-like glow shed on them by the nightlight. Her toes protruded in front, jammed close together like a single limb. She was leaning against the door, apparently lost in thought. There was a mysterious quality, a hidden grace, about her stance, the stillness and self-absorbed concentration of it. Sid leaned back against the window and watched her. Once again he thought he heard that piano: raucous, mawkish chords, like a children's tune run through the drive of a suction fan. The music mingled with the hum of the air-filtering system and was lost in it.

"Want some coffee?" The nurse had turned toward him.

He nodded, and went over to her.

"It's hot," he said.

The nurse wrapped her arms about her shoulders as though she felt cold. "I love the heat," she said. An attractive smile lit up her tired features.

"I can't stand it," said Sid.

"Without the heat there's no real summer."

"True," said Sid, smiling.

The nurse brought her left hand up to scratch the back of her neck, at the point where her bison's hump began, then dropped both hands to her sides. "I'll be right back," she said.

"Bro—"

"Yes?" he said, coming closer.

"Don't go."

"I'm here." He placed his hand on her forehead. She had no fever.

"Stay here with me, stay here tonight—" Her fingers hooked around his for a moment and went limp.

"All right."

"The thing that worries me is—" Sid began, when the nurse came back with the coffee. She carefully placed the hot mug in his hand. They were standing at the entrance to the ward with their backs to the wall.

"Is what?" she asked.

"Nothing really. I just keep wondering, um, why the doctor had that look on his face—" He took a sip of coffee that burned his throat.

"What look?"

"He didn't seem pleased that her temperature was down."

"I'm not sure," she said hesitantly. Sid looked at her in the half-light. Her skin was smooth and poreless, like plastic. "Doctors do say," she went on, unsure of herself, "that as long as there's a fever, the body's still putting up a fight, still resisting—"

"The body's still putting up a fight?" Sid repeated, but his mind was on something else. He had the feeling there was something he'd forgotten in the ward, some personal possession of his, or some unfinished business he had to take care of. But when he went back inside he couldn't remember what it was. Everything was quiet. Lia was asleep. The old lady was snoring gently. His sister's glass was still on the nightstand, with some wine left in it. Sid picked it up and drank the wine in one gulp. He saw the nurse return to the ward and scuttle quietly to her seat like a dormouse, without speaking to him. She pushed her stool against the wall and sat down. In a few moments she had fallen asleep, nodding back and forth every so often. Lia was breathing peacefully. Sid lightly caressed her hand as it lay on the sheet. He was still holding the empty wine glass. He put it back on the nightstand. Then he left.

The corridor was deserted. Only the head nurse's office had its lights on, and as he went by he saw her there, fast asleep, face on the table, arms hanging wearily at her sides. Sid walked to the elevator and pressed the call button. He heard the sound of the pulley starting up, and waited. The sound stopped. He looked at the red arrow: it had gone out. He pressed the button again. The light remained off. Sid pushed open the service door and saw the stairs in front of him. He started down them two at a time.

· 19 ·

*T*hree sevens are twenty-one," said Mama Koula thoughtfully. She looked through the window at the mulberry tree with its crooked whitewashed trunk, at the wire-netting fence, at the hayloft and the henhouse. Then her gaze shifted back to the kitchen. She studied the worn formica of the cupboards, the ancient squat refrigerator, the row of lustrous pots and pans hung on hooks above the sink. Finally her eyes settled on the floor tiles, gleaming in the morning sunlight.

"Yeah, and three eights are twenty-four," Sid responded, just to say something. Because he couldn't stand this minute scrutiny of every object in the place.

Mama Koula turned to him. "There are three weeks left," she said, as though doing a mental calculation. "Twenty-one days."

Across the strait the opposite shoreline was shrouded in mist. Sid stared at the bare yellowish mountain, its peak now hidden by clouds, its foothills firmly lodged in the sea. Bees were buzzing in the yard. Beyond the outstretched neck of the mulberry tree was a well that he hadn't noticed the last time he was there.

"I just don't know what to get done first," Mama Koula sighed. She got up from her chair and looked at him, waiting to hear his opinion.

"Oh, everything'll be just fine," Sid told her, with a stupid smile. He didn't know what else to say. He was still dazed from waking so early, and from the bus trip. Sotiris had called him the night before and had insisted on that he come out to the village, that he catch the first bus, that he pay for a taxi if need be.

"What's up?" Sid had asked him. Small cloud formations moving over India. Monsoon winds raging in Pakistan.

"Get yourself out here and you'll hear the whole story. Just leave at once." Sotiris was being cryptic.

Sid had been glued to the television screen, watching the weatherman as he discussed gale-force winds, flooding, and imminent disasters, all with the same vacant smile. What was going to happen in the Maldives? How strong was the wind blowing over the Galapagos group? This was the only thing occupying his mind.

"What did you say?" Sotiris had asked him after a while.

"All right, I'll come," Sid had replied.

And now, after a three-hour journey, packed in among soldiers and irritable housewives laden with shopping, his ears still ringing from the latest popular hits relayed full blast through the bus's loudspeakers, he was being told by Mama Koula that Sotiris was getting engaged. Could it possibly be to that little girl? The thought passed through his mind but he dismissed it. Not possible.

"Where's the mynah gone?" he asked, glancing around.

"Didn't you hear?" said Mama Koula, in surprise. "They took it to the vet. Sotiris says it's suffering from depression."

"Depression?" Sid burst out laughing.

"Animals understand everything. They've got a sixth sense, or whatever it's called now—especially our Maria, she's as sharp as they come—"

Can I be dreaming? Sid wondered. This interest of Mama Koula's in the deeper psychological recesses of birds left him speechless.

"You should have seen how she reacted," Mama Koula went on, with a dreamy look on her face. "If we'd let her she'd have clawed the girl to bits. You can't hide anything from her, she figured out right away that a rival had shown up—"

What's the real subject here? Sid asked himself. The hero listens to a stupid monologue and nods his head understandingly. Can he do anything else? Well, of course, he can get up and leave. But he doesn't, his chair's collecting cobwebs. And why? Because he obeys the needs of the story, the unfolding of the plot. Because he's following the inner rhythm. What rhythm? The one that'll give the figures free range to develop as characters. Because the hero's there to serve the story. That's what he has to do. And when the curtain falls, what becomes of the hero? Then he'll leave. He'll disappear into the wings. The hero'll become dust in the intense unbearable light.

"Black Magic!"

"You two know each other?" Sotiris asked, in surprise. He was holding the bird cage and standing in the middle of the kitchen.

"I'm Thanási," said his classmate.

"Julia," said Julia, smiling, and shook hands with him.

Is it possible they know each other? Sotiris wondered. He put down the cage, and for a split second was seized by a strange uneasiness. No, it's just one of Thanási's tricks, he decided. He just can't resist putting on some crazy act, some special thing of his own.

"And here's the prodigal daughter," Thanási was saying. He'd gone over to the cage, and sounded decidedly cross. "Look at me," he snapped. It was an order. "Look at me!" The bird hid behind its wing.

"Leave her alone," Sotiris protested, stepping forward. "She's—having problems."

"She needs a mate," Julia said. "That's what the vet told us."

But Thanási wasn't listening to a word of this. He knelt down in front of the cage, reached out his hand, and opened its door. "Come to Poppa," he said, in a voice as loving as a crocodile's.

What do we do now? Sotiris wondered. Good thing Julia was there. That girl had sound instincts. She too now approached the cage, stooping down on her high platform heels, and rested one hand on Thanási's shoulder.

"Sotiris tells me you were together in school."

"That's right, but the bird belongs to me," the classmate burst out, in a bizarre voice.

"No one's taken it from you," she said quietly, "and no one is going to."

The wind had changed direction, was blowing from the southwest. Amid the heat you could now distinguish a light breeze coming straight off the sea and breathing coolly on the back of your neck. Sid dragged a wicker chair into the yard and sat down. He stretched out his legs, closed his eyes. The last of the summer heat. His sister's last summer. Inside the house he could hear Sotiris and Julia talking. He couldn't make out what they were discussing. Plans related to their engagement? A small private wedding? A big public one with a reception?

"Where's the best man got to?" That was Mama Koula. No mistaking her voice.

No one answered her. Not a sound could be heard. Absolute silence. He couldn't handle that. It really got on his nerves. He half-opened one eye. A brisk breeze was blowing, yet the leaves of the mulberry tree didn't stir. Everything was quite still.

"Leave sheep to shepherds."

"I didn't say anything," said Mama Koula.

"Leave sheep to shepherds," the voice repeated.

"That's so cool." This from Julia. She sounded very cheerful. Accept all happiness from me and go. Leave me alone and take all happiness.

"Cool?" Now it was Sotiris speaking, in an irritated voice.

"Yeah, such a great expression, I mean—what your Dad just said about the sheep." Julia struggled to make herself clear. But she wasn't that good at explanations.

Everyone's forgotten the hero. He sits all alone in a yard, baking in the sun. Because the hero doesn't exist. Or rather, he exists to the extent that the story needs him. To provide a landmark, to bring out the inner rhythm. Until the characters come to life. After that he's of no use. One scene follows another, and he just sits there in his chair like some gaping idiot, watching. His hands are tied. He's useless, but he can't get away. What can he do, then? The hero back-tracks, dwindles, becomes one of the characters. Perhaps even the main character. And who's that? A moron. A hopeless moron, all set to burst into tears—what crap I'm sitting here dreaming up, Sid told himself. He kicked a pebble, and left his leg stretched out, toes spread inside his shoe. Behind him a bustle of activity was audible.

First out was Mama Koula, who rushed frantically past him, undid the latch, opened the gate, and hurried off. A minute later, Sotiris and his father emerged into the yard.

"We have some shopping to do, we won't be long," Sotiris said.

A few steps behind them came Julia, tottering along on her green high-heel sandals. She paused in the middle of the yard, thrust her head forward, and shook the hair back out of her eyes.

"I've missed you, Black Magic," Sid whispered. The same old crazy flame was blazing in his breast.

Her sharp-cornered face clouded over.

"Life is strange," she said. She scraped back her hair, tied it with an elastic band, and tried to smile at him.

"Come here—" Sid seized her hand and pulled her close to him. "Look, do you have any idea what you're doing?" This was his role. These were the words he had to say.

"I'm in love—" She told him.

A gentle breeze blew toward the middle of the yard. The parched leaves of the mulberry tree rustled faintly.

"Come here, I want to show you something."

He dragged her over to the henhouse, opened the door, and shoved her inside. Julia offered no resistance. They sat down on the straw, squashed close up one against the other. "Sid, Sid—" she sighed, but half-heartedly. Her face was expressionless.

There was only one fat white hen left inside. All the rest had gone out through the hatch and were clucking around their small wire-fenced enclosure.

He brought his mouth close to her ear.

"Want to daba dooba with me?"

"You know something?" she said, pulling away from him an inch or two. "He's different from the others." She put her hand to her nose. "It really smells awful in here—"

"Daba dooba? Just one last time?" he begged her.

She stared at him, frowning, in the semi-darkness.

"You're out of your mind—"

"Accept all happiness from me and go," he said.

He saw she was about to get up.

"My sister died," he told her.

"I'm sorry," she whispered, but he could tell from her tone of voice that she didn't believe him.

"She asked me to stay with her on the last night, but I left."

"I'm sorry," she said again, and her expression changed. "Is this all part of your daba-dooba act?" she asked sulkily.

"I left her there to die alone—"

"And now you have no one left in the world, is that it?" Her voice was mock solicitous.

"You don't believe me, huh?" He grabbed her by the shoulders and shook her.

"Let go of me—"

He threw himself on top of her, seizing both her hands. Then he pressed his face against her chest. He could hear her heartbeat. Two hollow thumps, then a deep silence.

"Let go of me, please—" She sounded on the point of tears.

His mouth sought hers. He bit her lower lip and sucked it in between his teeth. The taste of her saliva sent him wild. He grabbed her little breasts and squeezed them in his hands.

"You're crazy, I'll scream—"

"No one will hear you."

"Get him!" Mama Koula advanced cautiously toward the well. When she reached the low retaining wall she kicked off her slippers and ran barefoot through the mud. "Come back here, you hear me?" she told the rooster.

"What's going on here?" Sotiris's father shut the door behind him and marched out, heavy-footed, into the middle of the yard. "What's happening?" he asked again, with a questioning glance at Sotiris, who was ahead of him.

"You, get inside!" Mama Koula ordered the rooster. She stooped down, picked up a stick, and stretched forward to hit it.

"Stop," said the father. His tone of voice left no room for objection.

Mama Koula stood there hesitating for a moment, the stick still raised. "Get inside, you hear me?" she exclaimed, as she saw the rooster coming toward her. She turned around hastily, retreated two or three steps, grabbed one of her slippers, and took aim.

Sotiris watched passively. Down at the other end of the yard he saw Thanási, with a sour grin on his face, and Julia, who had turned her back on him. The rooster chase was of no interest to either of them. I have to do something, he thought. Those two really don't get along.

"Hold on!" he heard his father call out in a strangulated voice. Mama Koula stood there, the slipper still in her hand. Her husband hurried across to her. "You don't slaughter animals like that!" he told her, waving his arms. Mama Koula backed off. She was panting, her breast rose and fell. As she reached the fence she tripped, banging her head against a post, and collapsed on the ground in a heap, legs splayed. Her husband stared at her, speechless. Then he turned to Sotiris. "Get me the hose," he said.

I'm sick of you both, Sotiris thought. The way you're going on you're just humiliating me. He glanced at Julia, who was watching the scene in astonishment. She looked very upset. Her hair was mussed and there was a button missing from her blouse. I'll take you away, we'll get the hell out of here, he promised her silently.

"Get a move on!" his father shouted.

Sotiris bit his lip. He bent down and picked up the hose, took one last look at Julia, and got going.

"Look at the rooster," said Sid.

Julia turned back to him. Her brown eyes were full of suspicion.

"The rooster," he said to her again. There was a pleading note in his voice.

Julia turned and looked. On the lower part of her neck there was a bruise that his lips had left. The fuzz on her nape was dark and fluffy.

"Isn't he lovely?" Sid whispered behind her. They were only a single step apart.

"Lovely," she repeated, in an empty voice.

"Lovely, my ass," swore Sotiris as he hurried past them, dragging the hose. He went straight to where Mama Koula lay, still in a heap, and began to spray her face.

At the farther end of the fence his father could be heard muttering, "Where did that rooster get to?"

"Where did that rooster get to?" Sotiris repeated, the nozzle of the hose dripping in his hand.

Sid left Julia and strolled aimlessly around the yard. It was hot. As it got near midday the sun beat straight down on the stone flags. He'd moved some distance away from the others when he spotted the rooster. It was scratching around in front of the hayloft. Every so often its beak would peck at the ground in search of grain. Sid approached it. He stopped in the shade provided by the doorway of the hayloft, and waited. It struck him that the hunt for the rooster had assumed the dimensions of an ancient tragedy, and that very soon it would be his cue for action. Protected against the direct sunlight, he imagined himself standing tall, waiting, a rifle in his hands.

"Where did that rooster get to?" asked Mama Koula, who had come round, in an expiring voice.

No one said anything. Sid watched the rooster, now bent down over a tossed-out scrap of stale food, impatiently worrying at it. He saw its red comb bob up and down, agleam in the blinding light, the greenish reflections from its wings, the ebony sheen of its tail. And, directly behind the bright contour of its raised wings, he saw himself preparing to take aim. "Why don't we just off him?" he called out to the others. "Why don't we finish him off with a rifle and be done with it?" No answer. Sid took a few steps forward. He was in the middle of the yard, at the very core of the heat. Behind him, the flagstones around the well were steaming.

"Come here, all of you," ordered the father. The sun was now directly overhead, and there was no shade in the yard. Cicadas were chirring in the branches of the mulberry tree. Beyond the fence, thick smoke was rising from somewhere in the parched fields. "They're burning trash," said Mama Koula, as she got near him. "Over at the Tamvakoulas high rise."

Slow but sure, crest erect, the rooster moved in their direction.

"Everyone go to the well." By a series of gestures Sotiris's father conveyed to them that they all had to encircle the rooster, noiselessly, but not pounce on it until he gave the signal. The rooster was now less than a yard from them, and was still slowly coming on. Sotiris and Julia slipped behind it. The rooster strutted another couple of steps in the same direction, and then suddenly stopped.

"Get him!" the father yelled, the veins standing out on his neck. "Get hold of him, you fools!"

The rooster stood quite still in the middle of the yard, its eyes half closed. Suddenly it opened its left eye, and blinked.

"Uh-oh!" Mama Koula exclaimed.

What happened was what everyone had been afraid might happen, Sotiris reflected half an hour later, when the whole business was over and he was sitting peacefully in the yard with Julia in his arms. The rooster turned its attention to the henhouse, and crowed. Three hens arrived helter-skelter from behind the hayloft. The rooster went on crowing.

"What moron left the henhouse door open?" Sotiris's father raged. About a dozen hens were now circling the yard in a frenzied state. The rooster continued to crow. Sotiris's father grabbed a shovel.

"What moron—?" he bellowed again.

Sotiris had turned round to see if Julia was watching. She seemed hypnotized. Thanási, beside her, was taking in the scene with a sulky expression. In one swift movement, Sotiris's father raised his shovel and struck. A plump white hen collapsed on the ground without uttering a peep, its head half a yard from its body. Gushing blood filled the gap between them. Three other hens gathered round it. "He killed the broody hen, he killed her," wailed Mama Koula, and began to cry.

"Why couldn't we just eat the hen?" Julia asked. She'd come and put her arm around his neck, and was stroking him with velvet-smooth fingers.

"What?" Sotiris said.

"Why couldn't we have chicken soup instead of the rooster?"

"Mama Koula decides things like that," Sotiris sighed.

"Leave sheep to shepherds, right?" Julia said, laughing. He hugged her to him with all his strength.

The hen's blood, warm and red, poured out in the arena.

And after that? What happened then?

"Get him! Get him!"

The rooster stood stock-still in the middle of the yard, eyeing them. Once more Sid saw the whole scene as the unfolding of an ancient tragedy, once more he saw himself with a rifle in his hand, and prepared to take aim. He braced the butt against his right shoulder, and shut one eye. In the sunlight the bird's scarlet plumage glinted, turned green, azure, deep blue, and finally red again. Sid sighted his target and drew a deep breath. He was ready. Then some other bird abruptly entered his field of vision. A large, ugly bird with a nasty look. The weapon turned to dust in his hands.

"Hi there, Maria," said the mynah.

"Go get him, girl!" yelled Sotiris's father.

The rooster gazed in stupefaction at the black bird as it circled over its head, squawking.

The mynah as a *deus ex machina*. Now there's a story for my sister, thought Sid. And it seemed impossible to him that she wasn't alive to listen to it.

"Now!" exclaimed Sotiris's father, and raised his hand with the knife in it. Three minutes later he was on his way into the house, holding his winged booty by the legs. "Put some water on to boil," he told Mama Koula, and burst out laughing.

It was Julia's idea. It had gotten cooler, they'd gone for a walk into town, and had got as far as the central square. "Let's take some pictures," she suggested, and produced a small camera from her bag.

Accept all happiness from me. Leave me alone and take all happiness, Sid thought. "All right," he said, and smiled.

A bus was waiting at the side of the road, its engine running, spewing out dirty exhaust fumes.

"We forgot the mynah," said Julia.

"I'll go get it," Sotiris told her.

"No, I'll go." Julia ran off.

The two men were left there.

"She's going to try out for drama school," Sotiris said when she was out of earshot. "She wants to be an actress."

"She'll make it," said Sid.

The ghost of his sister, which was no ghost but his sister in flesh and bone and tight red shorts, went walking by, with a mischievous glance at him as she passed. She was with another older girl, and dragging a heavy worn suitcase. Without giving him another look, she handed over her suitcase to the baggage handler, and boarded the bus. Sid wondered whether Sotiris had noticed her, whether he'd recognized the kid. But his friend was looking elsewhere, in the direction Julia had gone, with a vaguely smug expression on his face.

Julia reappeared carrying the cage, smiling big smile.

"It's automatic," she said. She set the timer, and put the camera down on a café table. "Say cheese!" she called out, and ran to join them. Right. So, everything under control. The three of them stood there with their arms around one another, waiting for the click of the shutter. Sid was in the middle, holding the cage in one outstretched hand. The last things he remembered were Sotiris's stupid grin, Julia's big smile and crooked teeth, and his own lips, coming unstuck from his gums, leaving his mouth and making for his ears, before all three of them were enveloped in thick black smoke and everything disappeared.

The bus driver folded up his newspaper and shifted into gear. The bus moved off, wheezing with the effort. Nina had a seat in front, next to the window. She saw the three standing waiting at the corner of the square, all with big grins on their faces. The one in the middle looked like something the cat had dragged in: she'd noticed him earlier. Now he was clutching a cage with a black bird in it. The other guy, with the ears that stuck out, reminded her of something, she'd run into him somewhere before. The girl was a total freak. They were just standing there, petrified, as though they saw the end of the world coming and couldn't do anything to stop it.

"The zombies are taking photos," she said.

"Where?" Zoe leaned across to look, but a cloud of black exhaust fumes had swallowed all three of them.

As the bus jolted, Nina ran a finger lightly over her knee. The scar had faded, the cross was now invisible. Out the window, she saw the village's houses behind her shrink into a narrow tail and disappear. When it filtered onto the main highway the bus picked up speed and was on its way.

I am in the bus. I keep the balance with my mind. A direct, out of the blue trip. All the others are idiots and zombies because they can't see this. A bit to the right, a bit to the left. I can go wherever I like. I keep perfect balance and I advance. The bus glides forward on the shining highway. It follows a detour. It stops. It moves off again. It makes a sudden turn. It brakes. The bus speeds along on the silvery asphalt, speeds up and disappears. I don't care. I keep the balance with my mind. Mt. Paliovouna is vanishing. I can write whatever I like.

Author's acknowledgment

I would like to thank Gunilla Forsén and Lena Pasternak for their hospitality and warm support at the Baltic Center for Writers during April–May 1999.

—Ersi Sotiropoulos

Translator's acknowledgment

I would like to take this opportunity of expressing my heartfelt gratitude to Ersi Sotiropoulos for the constant help and encouragement she gave me during the course of this not always easy translation. She scrutinized every chapter with an unerring eye for detail; she was forbearing with my inevitable occasional misunderstandings of her highly idiomatic Greek; her own remarkable command of English led her often to find the *mot juste* when I missed it; and she always yielded the field gracefully when convinced that I was right and she was wrong. Our months of cooperation have been for me an invaluable seminar in the translator's art, and one I shall long remember with affection as well as gratitude.

—Peter Green